# FAT PEOPLE

# FAT PEOPLE

*A Novel*
*by*

Carol Sturm Smith

FICTION COLLECTIVE   NEW YORK

All of the characters in this book are fictitious.

Library of Congress Catalog number: 77-81004
ISBN: 0-914590-46-4 (cloth)
ISBN: 0-914590-47-2 (paper)

Published by FICTION COLLECTIVE
Distributed by George Braziller, Inc.
One Park Avenue
New York, N.Y. 10016

Acknowledgment is made to Carol Berge's *Center* #9 and
D. E. Steward's newsletter, *Sinter,* for publishing portions
of *Fat People;* and to The Ossabaw Island Project.

Special thanks to The MacDowell Colony, Peterborough, N.H.,
where much of this novel was written, and to Phillip Ramey for
"The Song of David," composed at my request for *Fat People.*

This publication is in part made possible with support from the
National Endowment for the Arts in Washington, D.C.

This publication is in part made possible with support from the
New York State Council on the Arts.

Grateful acknowledgment is also made for the support of
Brooklyn College and Teachers & Writers Collaborative.

Crossword puzzle and music artwork by Bonnie Bier.

*For Kristin Booth Glen, Susan Kleckner,*
*Jane Schroeder and Gloria Stern*

# PART I

"...females are fatter than males
at all ages."

— The Encyclopaedia Britannica

# Chapter One

Tomorrow I will be thirty-three. I will not reach the desert in time. Fuck. I drive beside Iowa grainfields. That is as gentle as it comes. We are in dry summer; it is August. The afternoon sun has done its job very nicely today; I toot it a pat on the head. Ahh, but the knot is at my core. *Still* not predictable, this rush from blood to viscera, cold and tight. It is more alive than memory.

What's the matter, you think being lonely should be a solitary matter?

It is hot, and I cannot sleep. The bed is a motel familiar; my flesh weighs upon me like a hundred unpaid bills; I am a cavernous mansion, burning in a summer downpour. I can no longer masturbate lying on my back. I am too old to learn new tricks..In the next room a couple makes love. They smack and crackle. I get up and find dimes for the candy machine.

They are still at it, my next-door neighbors, when I return, all ohs and ahs and small grunts now. Will they never be done? There is a mirror on the open bathroom door. I sit on the bed and contemplate my naked profile, head turned. I am like the scalloped edge of a pattypan squash.

The Mounds are indescribably delicious. In the next room, finally, there are murmuring sounds and soft bed creaks.


I will weigh one hundred sixty-seven pounds on my thirty-third birthday, an even thirty-three more than just three months ago. Very appropriate. I would say I am feeling guilty if anyone bothered to ask, because it would be expected. But I feel just a hard hollowness. Which is worse. It does not matter. What I do is what I do.

It is fierce, that New England place.

In the January cold, I took to staring in mirrors.

By May the men had come like trout fishermen moving along stocked streams.


I have lost my stand-by sex phantasies—they will not stay in place. I quest after food, as for the mother lode. Diner signs glitter; where are you, naked squirming friends? I am becoming a fat woman, ergo I am becoming jolly. I do not unzip and spring forth in a tutu. I wear my new rolls of flesh as memory aids. There is less baggage.


It is late afternoon, my thirty-third birthday. I send Will a postcard from Pipestone National Monument:

*August 24, 1971*

*A. Yes or no:*

*1. Being lonely should be a solitary matter?*

*2. If a friend is only seen smiling in bed, it is the duty of a friend to stop this activity altogether for moral reasons of a friend's own?*

> 3. *A friend could say something worse than*
> *"I'm not a prostitute" after a friend has*
> *offered to lend a friend some money?*
> B. *Fill in the blank:* _____

The waitress has unreal hair and a sullen look. She wears a plastic nametag above her left breast: Pearl. I ask for a menu and a glass of water. Pearl manages a scowl and brings the standard diner menu. No water.

The place reeks of inefficiency and stale grease. At the counter, a bowling foursome from some kind of plant complains. Ray, Mitzi, Adele, Sue. Hard, nasal voices, disappointed.

In the ladies' room, a soiled Kotex lies limp on the sink. It is brick red around a brown center. There are no paper towels. I do not wash my hands.

The food is unappetizing; I eat slowly. A bowler splits off from her companions and heads for the toilet. She returns, tight lipped, and stares at me coldly. She whispers to her team. Eyes gleam like dark boss marbles. My guilt is woman borne and eternal.

I register in a motel as Felicity Partridge. There is a color tv, and I green in the faces. I feed three quarters into the bed relaxacisor, and pour vodka over ice cubes. Rock Hudson and Doris Day square off. She loses.

I send Bailey a card from the South Dakota Badlands:

*August 30, 1971*

*Hi, Bailey: You'd like it here. It's a flesh lover's dream: pale white faces and deformities galore. At 167 lbs as of my birthday, I make it 6 out of 7 female plumpos here in the Ranger Station. You'd get some good*

*song lyrics out of this place. The Badlands
done be* very *weird.*

*XXX
TuTu La Grange
Alias Mouse #273*

It is cloudy, and there is fog. I am insulated in my car. The radio is full on and I smoke a joint. Quicksilver Messenger Service is singing *"What you gonna do about me?"* I convoy behind two rink-a-dink trucks carrying hogs, settle back in the seat. Red cardboard arrows push slowly out from ovaries, like the arrows in an air-conditioner display. They feel like felt. Beyond my glass walls, farms come and go through centuries. I drive on the road in a gray-green painted landscape. Ahead, there is a touch of color. It pulses and contracts, a bit at a time.

Speed converges in outer space.

Farting is a problem among mixed friends.

My thighs feel like birch twigs.


I pull into a roadside parking area and break out my hand drum. It is red clay, with a goatskin head. Before I even start my morning workout, I am joined by a large green travel trailer labeled "Daisy Mae" across the back in red letters. The side door opens. Four children tumble down the step as if released from church. I can not deal with that. I repack my drum.

Sweep talked of finding arrowheads when he was growing up Out West. His great grandmother had survived a fearsome Indian attack when she was just turned ten.

There must be secret places in the desert land where Sweep came from. The Indians had need to practice making voices with their drums. War rhythms drummed into the open air must carry very far. To have such power is a frightful thing. Did the master drummer teach young brave musicians in the depths of caves, perhaps? Or at the bottom of a steep-banked winding narrow dirt arroyo?

I send Sweep a postcard from Yellowstone National Park. It is a snapshot of Old Faithful, spurting against the sky:

*September 2, 1971*

*Dear Sweep: I have concluded, after six months of hard thought, that you were more willing to hang on to your saxophone than to hang on to our marriage. Strangely enough, I felt lonely and rejected because of this. You gave me permission to sleep with Will. I know you dismiss this as irrelevant, because only your position hardened. Toot-toot.*

*Sarah*

I pass a state mental institution. It sprawls by the side of the road. I park and play a little pick-the-patient. It is too warm for September, and the scene before me is lit by a Van Gogh sun. On one simple park-type bench, painted green, two women sit. One is a girl, perhaps eighteen, with toast-colored hair. It is tied simply at her neck, with a red bow. She wears a white blouse, navy skirt and sneakers. The other hides her face in a large hat; her dress is a print, a $9.95 chainstore special. It bulges. They are mother and daughter, side-show images.

Daughter sits quietly, her ankles crossed before her. Mother fidgets, as if for a creweled pillow to protect her from the hardwood seat. What does crazy feel like, calm or fidgety?

Will sends me Rick, the Young Viking.

They call at midnight from Will's studio, to invite me to a party.

"You've got to come over," the Young Viking says. "We're having a party." I can hear the lolita laughing in the room. How come her parents let her stay out so late?

"No."

"You've got to," the Young Viking says. "We want you here."

"Tell her she can come pose." Will has walked to the phone. He is easy to hear. The Viking laughs. "We've got dope and booze," he says. "Come on over."

"Let me talk to Will."

"She wants to talk to you." Raucous laughter. A jangle as the receiver is handed over. The *1812 Overture* is nearing its climax; the volume is turned up. Do they have *Bolero* stacked on the spindle?

"Come over, we're having a party," Will says.

I tell him it is late, which he knows, and that I am tired, which he doesn't care to hear.

"I can barely hear you," Will says.

"Turn the music down."

"Nope. This is the best part."

"Well, I'm not coming over."

"Okay. How about if I set you up? You said you want him."

"Sure."

I hang up. It is a May night, muggy, with noisy crickets. I squeeze an early mosquito between my fingers; it feels terrible. I take a quick shower but do not shave my legs.

It is 12:50.

The Young Viking reaches for the bed rungs behind my head, as Will does. It is softly humorous.

He works with phantasies, but I do not call him on it. Why bother? I have my own. He wants my legs around his, my hips to move faster. It does not matter what I do. He is fucking a chimera, using my cunt like a hand. He had gone upstairs to the bathroom, and not returned. Naked, he lay on my bed.

"Well, look at you," I say. He is beautiful. I reach to

kiss his mouth; he turns away. It is not that he wants. "Bad
case of dragon mouth," he says. There is pleasure in this
impersonal fucking. Surprise. I have an orgasm. It reminds
me of Nebraska.

It seems as if I summon them each time I work out on
the drum. One wears a light blue skirt, two inches below
the knee, and a white semi-tailored blouse; her hair is
auburn; it curls to her shoulders. The other has a sharp
nose and uneven pink-white lips. Both wear mesh stockings. Their shoes are open-toed and white.

"We heard your drum," the redhead says. She reminds
me of Rita Hayworth as a prison matron. She looks at Lips
for agreement. It comes.

They are selling Bible literature.

Hayworth speaks to me of Noah and the flood. Lips
nods vigorously; she moves her mouth silently as Hayworth
reads. There is a mosquito on Lips' forehead. Framed
between their heads is a new Pontiac convertible with a
white top. A third woman is at the wheel.

I give them a quarter and bid them good-bye.

Lips leers triumphantly. "We come by this way every
two or three weeks," she says.

In March, when the snow began to melt, I drove the
Porsche on the winding back road past the lake and over
the mountain, taking the curves hard and tight. The road is
narrow. I caught up with a Mercedes convertible; a man
was driving; he speeded up; I stuck to his tail. The road lifts
and dips and then widens. I shifted down and went by. He
gave me the sign: pretty good, for a chick. I gave him the
finger.

Sweep and I were mated for five years, part of the time
married. I played housewife, and he played his saxophone.
He took me into the woods; I had not been there before.
Often, we made love. He said I was beautiful. I thought he
was the sun.

An astrologer friend said we should have known, I being a Virgo, he a Sagittarius. It took us a while. I was used to being used; he wasn't the fucking kind.

Where are you, my unborn children?

I have left my satchel of gris-gris in a quarter locker.

I stop at a pizza joint and order a pie with extras and a couple of Cokes so that the clerk won't know the pie is just for me. I drive for many miles. I cannot find a motel. The Porsche windows are up against the evening mountain chill, and the smell wins. I pull into a roadside rest area. A battered blue Volkswagen camper with drawn madras curtains is parked at the far end.

A single naked bulb throws yellow light onto a single dark green garbage can. The hinged lid is chained to a post. It reminds me of an alligator's jaws.

I salt the pizza and dig in. I eat two pieces whole and wash them down with Coke. I select an anchovy to nibble on, a hunk of cheese without the crust, a piece of sausage. I watch a car cruise on the road. It pulls past. It slows. It stops. It turns. Returns.

Cops.

I am indecently exposed.

Will plotted the taking of the lolita's cherry as if he were Alexander. We had meetings, Will and I and Rick, the Young Viking. I thought it was a nice fun game; toot-toot.

"Humbert," I say, "what if she falls in love with you."

"She won't."

"Yeah, she might," Young Viking says.

Will paces the studio. I am stoned and vaguely drunk on bourbon and gingers. He flashes in the spotlight that illuminates his Linus Pauling working model; it is a camera shot. I turn my head away. Young Viking has put a John Coltrane album on the stereo. It is one of Sweep's

favorites. He spent weeks learning Trane's solo on the
second cut.

"That would be heavy," Will says finally.

Young Viking and I agree. That is easy.

"Nah. It'll be good for her. I won't let her get involved.
Sleep with her three or four times, that's all. Even if it gets
heavy, it's better than letting some seventeen-year-old jerk
pop her."

"I think that's true," I say.

"Who am I to disagree with a woman?" Young Viking
says.

"Who wants to come over later?" I say.

It was getting heavy.

The toilet leak had filled the catch pan. It is the big
heavy-duty aluminum one I use to make soups for
company. The water needs spilling over the edge of the tub.
Which is worse, a toilet's drip-drip or a tub with a slow
drain?

"Hey, would you come upstairs and give me a hand
with this?"

There is a scar. It piques me. I lean to touch it, my
mind on Will's long, blunt, sculptor fingers. *You can't
always get what you want, but if you try, sometimes you get
what you need.*

Is there a sheet to put on the bed? No.

He is Ernest Broadman, a potter, newly moved to
town, newly married, sleek and lean, tanned, in his early
thirties. He has come to sell me some grass. A girl made the
scar with a broken glass, he said, turning his arm to let
light on it. I ask if she meant it, and he said, yes she did,
she's something else.

"I'm something else."

He laughs and reaches to kiss my mouth. I turn my
head into the pillow. We laugh to different drums. My
clean towel lies sacrificed to my bathroom leak. Fucking
gunk oozes onto the mattress cover.

"I'll get a towel," Ernest says.

I pick up his shirt from the floor and gently wipe his penis and thighs; it is less trouble than the laundromat.

I think I am in Wyoming. Will I never reach the desert? I stop in a market and buy some Ayds and a large bag of marshmallows. I register in a motel as Phemele F. Martin. In the next room, a couple fucks. I unwrap a glass and listen in at the wall. They are very talkative. I eat the Ayds; they taste good.

The tube yields a Cincinnati-Mets game. Ed Kranepool boots an easy grounder back of first. I switch the channels and catch six minutes of local commercials.

The hangers are attached to a bar in the closet, and will not come off. I get a fork from the car. I impale the marshmallows by twos. The management has thoughtfully provided matches. Sometimes I eat the burnt part from the outside and relight the whites. They taste like cake icing. I like to decorate cakes, to make fluff from fluff.

I met a man in August in the Howard Johnson's near Concord, Mass. He looked like a farmer, an undangerous man. He was a writer of biography. He was in his early fifties, and badly married. He said I looked like a Rubens painting, with my thick dark hair and radiant flesh; he reminded me a bit of Sweep.

I have an image, of a small girl child, dressed in pink. She is walking through the acre flower garden and orchard I have let grow wild, coming back from the town lake. She nears until I see her wide eyes, as blue as irises. She sees me then, and hurries to the window. She is smiling. I smile back. She reaches up and bangs on the screen. It topples.

It was as inevitable, that I would let that man come to my bed. I am a collector of experience. I have seen it on the soap operas.

He was in better shape than I, his body strangely firm. It was good. He stayed one night. I brought us Brie and crackers, grapes and wine in glasses on a pewter charger.

He killed a wasp. That he was making love seemed tolerable.

In the morning I woke refreshed. There was a moment of tenderness. He fell down the steps and was dead when I joined him at the bottom. Shit.

*September 12, 1971*
*Boulder, Colorado*

*Dear Will:*
*Sorry about the lower right-hand side.*
*No wonder you couldn't find the solution:*

*Sarah*

I am overcome by the leanness of my accomplishments.

# Chapter Two

I had a loop inserted. Oh my dear god. I spend the day in Purgatory: Sandra, the ex-Salvation Army drummer, comes to put a cold towel on my forehead and empty the vomit pan. She is a friend of Ernest's bride and has been distant. There are things I want to tell her, but I can not. She fusses with the bedding; I retch. It is good that she leaves; past midnight, in a dark hour, I remember the grass and at last there is rest.

In the morning I am weak. I have traded one day for the many of forgotten pills. I claim a low pain threshold. Perhaps this is not true. Is it death I am testing?


"How many men have you slept with?" Will says.

"Forty-six," I tell him. It is a Joseph McCarthy figure, shifting with my whims.

Will narrows his eyes. He pats a piece of clay in place. "Old demon flatness got me again," he says. "You've put on a couple of pounds." His head is askew; his mouth tightens. A brave director would risk an eyepatch, or a well-chewed thin cigar.

"Too few or too many?" I say. I can not restrain myself. I am lying naked on the purple velvet modeling couch in his studio.

"Enough," he says. "I'm tired. Want a drink?"

"Sure."

He makes us gin and tonics. He squeezes juice from a fresh lime. "Tell me about the kinky ones," he says. He has been mixing bourbon with his gin and tonics and is drunk. That is best. In the morning he will not remember and gloat. He takes me on the canvas mat.

Both thighs have chafed, high up near my crotch. I itch. It is uncomfortable. I register in an Aspen motel at three in the afternoon. I have brought a box of Drake's coffee cakes, whipped butter, a jar of Spanish olives, Triskets and sardines in mustard sauce, a half-pound of fresh-sliced provolone, a *National Enquirer,* a cold quart of Coors. I check out the damage—I have worn my skin red-raw. There are welts. I ooze yellow stuff. Do I have the clap? I do not dare attempt a bath. I fear an inability to rise. I shower and wash cautiously; it helps.

My wardrobe is in terrible shape. I cruise the streets until I spot a thrift shop. I buy the things that fit me comfortably: a raincoat with a warm lining, a pair of heavy blue denim pants—will the crotch turn green?—a spiffy pair of black nappy pants with an elastic panel in the front, a delicious red and green checked housedress that makes me look like a tent and a couple of blouses, one white with ruffles and one pink flowered with a bib. They remind me of my fifth-grade teacher, Miss Montclair the Mountain. I haggle the salesgirl down to $3.50. I donate my old clothes to the shop. I take a tax deduction slip for $16.75, "In the Name of Irma McHoole."

I bag Hargrove Millious, the local plumber. He is badly married, too, like the one I met near Concord. Do they hatch in the spring like black flies? We sneak on a back road and make it on the front seat of his station wagon as teenagers do. He has been betrayed by a true love; I listen. It is a fine gift he had offered.

"How many men have you slept with?" Hargrove says.

I consider. "Seven," I tell him.

He tests his crotch like an old man in baggy pants at a funeral.

He worries about his reputation.

I try the old whore trick, give him a couple of tokes of pot and go down. It works.

Young Viking flunks out on a night when I really need him. Will has been in New York for a week reviving contacts. I call Young Viking at the studio. He is setting up the armature for Will's Linus Pauling sculpture.

"How about some company?" I say. "I've got to get out of the house. I'm going nuts. The place is a frigging mess and I don't know what I'm doing."

"I'm not in the mood," he says.

Fuck you, you john.

Joan Broadman goes to a Boston abortionist and gets in trouble. She is hospitalized. I do not understand why Ernest and his Bridie took that course of action. They have been married less than half a year. They have bought the large grey house with sixteen wooded acres behind Sam the guitar maker's place and put in a kiln.

It is their decision.

I go to keep Ernest company.

Ernest makes his living throwing cups and vases, plates and bowls, and rolling slabs of clay to cut and shape and glaze for mirror frames and ashtrays. For fun he makes strange vaguely human shapes. He is going to populate his woods. He takes me to the first, a female form with foxy head reclining nude by the base of a dead sugar maple with a tap and pail in place.

"That's Elizabeth Taylor," Ernest says.

The figure bears grapefruit breasts. It is smaller than life. "That's pretty weird," I say.

"Observe."

Elizabeth's legs are hinged and Ernest opens them. He whittles a pointer and gives a lecture. "You will notice here

a slight protuberance which should in no way be confused
with anything living or even simulating life...." He is very
funny.

I stay for three days and two nights. Used dishes
remain in the sink. Ernest does not complain. Toot-toot.
We take an acid trip and make fine music. Ernest plays a
wicked banjo. I have brought my drum. In candle light,
with the space outlining the body of my drum contained by
the tightener thongs, my drum looks to me like a mandrill's
head. The color is not right, of course, because a male
mandrill's face is streaked with blue about a bright red
snout that sometimes looks like a fine tough cock erecting
from red nostril balls, and the clay of my drum when it
talks to me is the color of soft bricks in late afternoon
sunlight, but shape devoid of color is suggestive.

My first after-loop period lasts a week and a half. It is
heavy, with clots. There are cramps; I had thought I was
done with those in my teens. The odor is rank. I buy an
aerosol feminine hygiene spray. It is miserable stuff. I am
horny all the time. I need to be made love to; I will settle for
being fucked. Hargrove the local is aghast at the sugges-
tion. He blushes at the word menstruation. I wonder how he
is on adultery. My will power is not what it should be. I call
Will; he says to come over. He is in his livingroom reading
*The Sunday New York Times*, several days late. He is still
at it several hours later. There is a dampness between my
legs. I have bled through my super Tampax. I make a
substitute with a toilet-paper wad and stuff it in.

Will is reading the classified ads.

"Jesus H. Christ."

"What's the matter now?" he says.

"What do you mean 'now?'"

"You've been grouching all evening."

"How would you know, you've had your nose in the
*Times* ever since I arrived."

He slams the paper on the couch. "You're the
moodiest damn female I've ever seen," he says.

"You're uptight about my period."

Will snorts. "And that makes you uptight, right?"

"Right."

He snorts again. Perhaps I am wrong. I reflect. I am right.

It is after midnight before we go upstairs. Will is not one to shirk his responsibilities. He has trouble coming. He has plowed in with no foreplay. There are slurping sounds. I control my laughter. He buries his head in the pillow and humps away. By the time he makes it I no longer see the humor. Will goes to the bathroom. Water runs in the sink. He is washing. It is not his habit.

When he returns, I feign sleep. In the morning there will be a bloody mess. I find my satisfaction in the thought.

I send Mick Jagger a postcard from The Flaming Gorge National Recreation Area:

*September 22, 1971*

*Dear Mick Jagger:*

*I have been thinking about your song, "Let It Bleed." At least I think it is your song.*

*In any event, although I do not believe it is exactly what you had in mind, it occurred to me today that sixty days a year my cunt juice is unacceptable. I have not been gone down on when I menstruate. There is a gagging double standard. Sperm isn't exactly cherry jello.*

*Furthermore, what is love all about, anyway?*

*Yours truly,*

*Sarah Gorge*

I doodle 3-dimensional boxes on a napkin. Clusters of grapes. Rectangles. I am in a restaurant, waiting for my food. The sign said, *September Special, $2.19*. A bargain. The special is a rib-eye steak. I order mine medium rare. I am not quite the only customer. It is 3:15 in the afternoon.

"The chef said if this is too well done, send it back. He

overcooked it." The waitress stands at the table and waits for me to test the steak. It is a single step up from Eastern Airlines' mystery meat. It is badly overcooked.

"It's all right," I tell her.

The cashier wears a black string tie with a discreet silver and turquoise pull. He wears a pinkie ring on his left hand. His smile resembles the gristle left on my plate. "You're a long way from home," he says. His cheeks withdraw above jowls.

"That's right."

"I saw your license plate," he says. "I grew up in Boston. Do you live near there?"

"A couple of years away."

Why is he looking at me so strangely?


On the first Friday night in February, three weeks before Sweep split for good, I took Will to be my lover. It is the straw. It was flesh I sought, a specimen trophy to stuff and dangle. I shuffled possible consequences, tossed them into a cranny. How inconsequential they proved, Plato shadows in a shark tank. I have developed calluses working out on the drum. They do not apply. I get sick in the mornings; I am pregnant. It has taken two years. I get it sucked out.

Will has an attack of hindsight. He claims his involvement was in the coupledness of my marriage. It is not easy to hear; the child was not his; he had preened and offered himself. I asked for no commitment.

There is time to be generous.

"More," he says.

"Fellatio? Is that how you pronounce it?"

"I think so."

I get the after-abortion go-ahead from the legal clinic in New York. I want to use myself. Will burdens me.

"What do you want?" he says.

"I want to get laid."

"No. You want more than that. I want you to know

I'm as involved now as I'm going to get. I'm not in love with you."

I tell him I know this, that it is mutual. He takes me less than seriously. Can't he see that I mourn?

For a month, while he is working on the sculpture that he makes of me, Will puts out with his fingers and tongue and cock; it is worth the endless daylight, these nearly nightly sweaty feasts. We both booze more each one. He says I could kill a man. It is not my intention.

"I should find you another lover," Will says.

"What about Rick? He looks like a Young Viking stud. He assists you with your other work."

Will laughs. "That's not a bad idea. His cock is something else, by the way."

"I can take it. I'm something else."

"You are indeed."

Full-moon eve he sends Young Viking.

Full-moon night he comes to me.

"Some haul," Will says. "Rick the Young Viking and Will the Bull in the same day. Pretty lucky chick. I'd say that's an eight-and-a-half on a ten scale. Not bad, for a mediocre lay."

"I've got an idea. Why don't you pop the lolita and train her to do what you want."

"Good idea. Why don't you make us some food. I'm hungry."

"Fuck you."

He grabs and brings me close. "Actually, it doesn't matter. I just wanted to get laid. You're worth a short drive."

*Come on, take another little piece of my heart now....*

I gain six pounds in May, another seven in June. It is a beginning.

I make it to the remnants of a Colorado gold-mining town. The altitude is nearly 10,000 feet. It is hard to drive. The Porsche is feeling sluggish. My ooze is wetter and the itch worse.

I find a doctor. I weigh in at 181 pounds. I have vaginitis. Shit. I will go forever without the clap. The prescription fills a box half the size of a carton of cigarettes. Will I be dropping these pills in my grave?

I stop at a diner. It is also a truck-stop motel. The waitress doubles as the office. The food is cheap and plentiful. I register as Hilda Baumert.

The motel room is a horrid-smelling cubicle. There is a single window high above the bed, a towel on a plain wood chair, a radio on a nighttable. The carpet is walk-up apartment hall green.

I open the pill box. It contains yolk-yellow ovals the size of robin eggs. There is a plastic plunger for insertion. I finally get one in. It is more trouble than a diaphragm.

In the morning I wake with sticky thighs and matted pubic hair. The sheet is badly stained. I toss it in the corner. The mattress is worse than the sheet. The toilet is in the diner. I put on the white blouse with ruffles and my denim pants. I pull the tab. The zipper breaks. I close the opening with a pin. I walk the gauntlet in the diner. I am becoming more invisible with every pound I gain. A man in his mid-forties, carrying a towel and newly clean, is coming from the mens' toilet. He is about 5 feet 10 inches tall, wiry, and his lithe walk reminds me of Sweep. His eyes are as green as Bailey's. There is no toilet paper in the womens' lavatory. I use my towel. How come there is a shower for the men and none for me? I complain nicely. The waitress is impressed. I wait a half an hour for my breakfast.

I lived with Sweep for a year before we were married. I gave him that name. It is short for Sweetie-pooh. Ugh. We were married at City Hall. I needed the paper; I thought it would unlock my 10¢ dream toilets. Another freebie. Toot-toot.

We order up wine and make some calls to Sweep's musician friends. I put up a chili bean hodgepodge and some batter breads. The loft is a mess. I toss things into drawers and empty ashtrays into the fireplace. It is a noisy crowd. Sweep breaks out his saxophone. There is a nice fat jam. I keep the glasses filled with wine and make four pots of coffee. There is enough grass to keep the Principality of Liechtenstein stoned for a month, and Bailey has brought an ounce of hash as a wedding present. He has found a new dealer, a crazy woman who collects shrunken heads. Things break up at dawn; we are too tired to make it.

In the late afternoon, after we sleep off the wine and smoke, Sweep gets on a kick about the dirty dishes. Fuck, fuck, fuck. I crawl under the covers in a tight ball. *Life would be a dream, shaboom....*

There are voices in my drum; I caress the smooth tight skin and it responds to me. It is urgent and demands. There are changes to be made. I hold the center together. It is a puzzle of multitudinous levels. Perhaps I can extract and sell it to Parker Bros.

I had an urge to play my drum with Sam, the guitar maker. That is not quite true. It is sex I want, but playing my drum with Sam and his guitar will do. It is worth a try. It is eleven o'clock on a Tuesday evening. The voices in my drum are talking well to me tonight. My fingers feel like raw meat.

Will's house is not even on the way. I drive by anyway. I decide to stop. I do not have my wits about me.

"I'm working, Sarah. This is a bad time."

"Good-bye."

Will starts to close the door.

"A-ha!" I point. Over the back of a chair in the diningroom is the lolita's jacket. It is red corduroy.

"It's not how it looks," Will says. He steps outside.

"Sure, Will. I understand."

"Come on, Sarah, don't be like that. She's a good kid."

"Does that mean you did it?"

"Yes." Will gets a sheepish grin. "No," he says, "she won't do anything but pet."

"Too bad."

"I thought you were leaving."

"I thought you had more sense."

"What does sense have to do with it?"


Sandra, the ex-Salvation Army drummer, disturbs me.
She spends her days emptying bedpans for her arthritic
Mama. She reads child psychology. On windy days she
covers her short dark hair with a white scarf. She would
make a Hepburn nun. We talk about masturbation. She
feels guilt. Who doesn't? She is a non-fucking virgin. You
can take the drummer out of the Army, but....

She arrives on a Thursday morning at nine. She is
obviously shaken. I splash water on my face and make
coffee. She has been the night before to a woman's group
for the first time.

"Every one of them confessed to having a sexual
problem," she says. "I don't want to be involved with such
messed-up people."

"And you don't have a problem?" I say.

"I'm a virgin."

"That's not a problem? You're twenty-eight."

"Twenty-seven. Why are you attacking me?"


My local and I come off together. I would not have
known, he is such a silent man. It is a first for him; he is
clearly pleased. We talk. He had thought it a myth. He can
not believe I come so soon and often. He is right. It is an act
of mercy. A groan. A grunt. A shiver. I am the hot-blooded
Jew girl of his dreams. It keeps him going. One is enough
for me.

"Is that all right, to call you a Jew? I've never known
one well enough to ask," Hargrove says.

"Sure."

Why not?


There are a few that get away. Sam, the guitar maker,
for instance. I do what I can. I tell him I am horny.

"Christ, Sarah, I think what we have goes beyond sex, don't you?" Sam says.

"No."

He looks me in the eye and smiles. "Friendship is at best a compromise."

"I say yes and you say no. Where's the compromise?" I say.

He reaches for his guitar and tries to soothe me with some music.

"How about some music?" I say.

"Sarah, sometimes I just don't understand you."

What's not to understand? "What's not to understand? I want to fuck and you don't."

"Well, that doesn't mean we can't be friends, does it?"

Young Viking calls me at home. He wants to come over. I take a snack upstairs; there are crackers crumbs on the sheet. We will have a quickie in the hot room under the attic eaves.

He undresses and kisses my forehead. We work up a sweat. It feels good. Viking is done and dressed; I do not complain. He takes the stairs by twos. I suspect I hear him whistling. I masturbate. Toot-toot.

Lips and Hayworth return. They have been driven in a white Lincoln. Business must be good. Fine. I need not feel guilty for keeping them out. I hold the screen door closed and plead work. Their smiles are hollow. I suspect they've heard that one before.

There is a black bug in my split pea soup. It is half hidden beneath a crouton on my spoon. It is dead. Drowned, I presume. I am in a Mormon diner, not too far from Bryce Canyon. I have taken a corner booth, easy to maneuver. I summon the waitress.

Over the back of the booth before me, the head and torso of a little girl appears. She looks to be four. She stands on the seat eyeing me, face solemn. Beside her is the misshapen gauze-covered head of her mother; the mother's hair is in rollers. A father and an older brother are also present.

The waitress is small and tidy. I show her the bug. She grimaces in distaste and apologizes. I cancel the soup. I have small hope for the rest of the food.

The little girl kicks the seat and jumps a bit. She is restrained by her mother. She disappears.

My fried shrimp come. They are tasteless. Southern Utah is very far from the sea. What am I doing? There are rolls in a wicker basket, wrapped in a paper napkin. They are cold. The little girl reappears and quietly watches me eat. Her eyes follow the movement of my fork. I stare at her.

"You are a fat one," she tells me.

"I know."

She disappears abruptly. There is a shrill reprimand, the sound of a slap. Why? She had only told the truth. The little one is crying still as the adults collect the check and bundle the children into coats. The mother smiles at me apologetically. They leave in a flurry and reassemble in a large car parked directly outside the window of my booth. The children are strapped in the back seat. It would make a nice campaign: *The family that belts together* dot dot dot dot. I wave at the little girl. She turns her head away.

*Oct. 11, 1971*
*Shiprock, N.M.*

*Hi, Bailey: I have left a trail of yellow gunk-puddled motel sheets behind me, thanks to some incredible suppositories a doctor prescribed for an attack of vaginitis: Hannah Jean Ogilvy took Leadville. Eloise Greenberg struck in Grand Junction. Lois Mallory did it to Fruita. Linda Bartless glopped near Arches National Monument. Sonya Paliskety and Billis R. Pillory hit near The Canyonlands. Eustace Lowenstein slept near Bryce Canyon and (Mrs.) Laura Llewellyn*

went to Zion. Lorraine Kraft took Kanab by
storm. The Grand Canyon is very big. Sarah
Baisley Farfell left her mark. This country is
grand and colorful. Too bad all I can see is
yellow. I'm on an incredible trip. I've put on at
least another 10 pounds. Spending a lot of money
on a lot of crap. There are occasional moments of
clarity, like now, but mostly there is a kind of
numbness, as if the half year from the time Sweep
split until I split is my only reality. I can't even
think about Sweep. I don't understand what
happened, why I can't control this incredible self-
destructiveness. I know its self-destructive, but
that doesn't seem to matter at all. I eat, and I
drive, and I turn on, and I eat, and I drive, and I
check into a motel and I drink and there you are:
you and Will and Young Viking and Hargrove (I
didn't tell you I was sleeping with him, too) and
Ernest and the one nighters and the horrible pig-
faced man I saw at the county fair who was
literally drooling at some side-show women who
were reflected in his mirrored sunglasses. Ugly,
ugly, ugly. There is a road out here in Indian
country lined with beer bottles. Miles and miles
and miles of beer bottles, some kind of desperate
message. We really did them in. I've been playing
my drum, but I'm looking for a place somewhere
in a canyon to really let it go. I did some target
practice with the pistol the other day. Hap-pi-
ness is a warm gun, bang bang, shoot, shoot. It is
all in the aim. Why should it feel easier to shoot a
gun than to play a drum? I haven't been able to
find the voices in my drum for quite a while now.
It scares me. I have no destination in sight.
People here call this the desert, but it doesn't look
like the desert to me. There isn't any sand. Who
ever heard of a desert without sand? I'm sorry this

*is such a downer, but it's good to know that you are out there for me to dump it off on. Do you realize we've been friends for nearly 10 years? That's nice, isn't it.*

*Sarah*

# Chapter Three

Sandra has come through. I pick up my mail in Taos. Bill. Next. Bill. Next. Bill. Next. Belated birthday greetings from Cousin Rachael, my only living relative. It is a rendering of a sweet bouquet and says, "To My Favorite Cousin On Her Birthday." Bill. Next. Sweep's lawyer must have had a hey-day with the letter. A legal separation. Slash slash. I'd like to meet the head that dreamed that little doozy up. I'll bet he's forty-one, a paunchy balding glass-eyed German Jew.

I check into a motel. I have brought a bottle of bourbon and an assortment of junk from a grocery store, a Morton's frozen chocolate cream pie, a bag of potato chips, a pre-packaged torpedo sandwich, a bag of licorice bites.

I pace the room. Twenty-two steps, and I have made a full circle. The roll of flesh that has replaced my abdomen undulates. It is solid and will not come off easily. It is protection. I will cling to it.

We are to play poker. Will has invited Sandra; Young Viking; Ernest and the Bridie, now recovered from her abortion; Sam, the guitar maker. I am tempted to suggest my local. It is too dangerous. Will is cunning. I need have my secrets.

Will thinks himself an adult. He has lost his fear of premature ejaculation. Too bad. We fuck. I have come early and made us dinner. The others arrive. We keep them waiting.

Will makes us noisy by pulling on the bed rungs. There is occasional laughter from Young Viking below. Will pauses at the bottom of the stairs to pound his chest and bellow a jungle yell. The men howl. I dally. It is the solitariness I savor.

"Sarah, get your tail down here. Let's play poker."

It's only time. I pull on my clothes and go to join them. *Well, you roll through the morning, they roll you through the night and day.*

It is dinky stuff, the game. We play for pennies and nickles. There is good humor of the sort found in ball-park bleachers. Who needs it? Joan Broadman is a blue-eyed blonde. Sandra is an ex-Salvation Army drummer. She cannot shuffle. What could be expected? We drink beer. There is much bathroom traffic. The acoustics are interesting in Will's house. Young Viking flushes before he has finished urinating.

I suspect Sam has a small prick. He hides behind his beard and holds his cards close to his chest. Does he jerk off at night and wad it in a wash cloth? He is my odd man out.

There is a clamor for food. I am elected. It is Will's house. Am I being charged for the conspicuousness of my winnings or for Will's climax? Never mind. I put together sandwiches and a bowl of pretzels and chips.

Ernest has won twice while I was gone. That figures. It is getting late. Five card draw. A small pot. Just Bridie and me. She folds on the last two-cent bet. Stupid cunt. The men are busy with the food. She shows her hand. It is good. She asks if I am bluffing. There is a sudden hard look to her face, a tightness around the eyes; is she calling the bigger bluff?

"That's what you pay to find out," I say.

Will has been watching after all. He snakes out a hand

and exposes my cards. Club king, jack, seven, four, spade deuce.

I lose even when I win.

I pound my chest and give a jungle yell.

The black flies will not go away. They attack in swarms. Their bites raise itchy red hives. The local laughs at my discomfort.

"You get used to it," he says.

I doubt it very much.

There are notes in my drum I have not heard before. They are hidden in the center and the edges. I have warmed up to look for them. Lips and Hayworth pull a three-year-old blue Falcon into my driveway.

Lips is wearing a leopard-skin pillbox hat with a stick-up veil and a plain black dress with a little white scalloped collar.

"Hello." Hayworth's voice is high-pitched, inflected and pleasant. "We would like you to have the new issue of *The Watchtower*," she says.

"I'm sorry. I'm really not interested."

"Have you read it lately?" Lips smiles an offer of hot rhubarb pie and comfort.

"All right. I'll take one." It only costs another quarter.

They make a U-turn from the driveway, tires squealing. Oh shit, I've done it again.

I am playing solitaire. I like the simplicity of the game. Either you win or you lose. I nearly play out a hand. It makes me as nervous as a mosquito invasion. I have set a limit. One more win and the game is over. The door bell is pulled. Toot-toot. I could stand a bearded stranger. I collect the cards before I go.

"Hello there, Tobias Paley Gorsham the Third."

"Hi, Sarah," Bailey says.

The oval horrors are as effective as a dermatologist's

salve. I plunged them in faithfully, one by one, according to direction. The itch returns. The ooze strikes again. I have been here before. I am in Durango. I make the rounds of burger joints and check into a motel as Mrs. Lydia Goldham. I smoke a joint. My stash is getting very low.

I check the yellow pages and call a gynecologist. I explain the situation. I ask for directions to his office.

"Where are you?" he says.

"Colorado. In the merry month of June."

"It's October twenty-fifth," he says.

I find the office anyway.

I weigh in at 187 pounds.

He tells me I have vaginitis.

I tell him that I know this.

He gives me a prescription to fill.

Flat white suppositories.

Men.


"How many men have you done that with?" Will asks.

"Nine."

"What do you do, keep score in a little black book?"

"Yes."


Sandra calls. She wants to go to a movie. I put her off for a while and check out Will. He is working on his Linus Pauling sculpture. Young Viking isn't home. Ernest's Bridie and the local's wife are.

We go to the drive-in to see *Love Story*. I have brought a joint. It helps a lot. It makes Sandra nervous. Leukemia, for Christ's sake. How about breast cancer that's spread? Sandra has not brought Kleenex. No one can accuse her of thinking ahead; she might have been an ex-wife.


My local has gotten bold and foolhardy. I am all he has ever hoped for.

"You're the first woman I've slept with I'm not in love with," he tells me.

I recognize the line; I have heard it on occasion before.

"How many women have you fucked?" I ask him. He
does not like to hear me use the word. He thinks it belongs
to men telling dirty jokes in beer joints.

"You're the third."

The third, for Christ's sake! He is twenty-nine. There
is still time for him. He would come to the back door of my
house each night. *Kind woman, don't leave me lonely
tonight.*

He begins to cramp my style. Where was he when I
needed him? I am tired of stories of the true love who
betrayed him and of his dreary wife. Especially his wife.
Her apron strings are long.

"Are you still sleeping with Will?" he says.

"Yes."

"I wish you wouldn't."

"I'm not going to tell him about you."

"No. That's not what I meant," he says.

He will explain. I get us some booze. I'll probably need
it.

"My wife would be very angry if she gets the clap," he
says.

Cock sucker.

An Englishman comes. He has rented a cottage on the
lake for two weeks.

"Look, I cahn't get involved with you sexually," he
says.

"You are involved with me sexually. We spent last
night in bed getting your cock up."

"No. I've got a set-up at home."

"What does that have to do with anything? She's there
and you're here and I'm here. It didn't matter last night,
why does it matter today?"

"She's in love with me."

"What does that have to do with our sleeping
together?"

"Look, don't do this. It isn't right. You're trying to
make me feel guilty. There is no reason for it."

"What do you mean there isn't any reason for it? I trust my feelings. My feelings tell me I'm getting fucked over. I don't like getting fucked over. It makes me angry."

"Well, you're crazy. I haven't done anything to make you angry."

Will is enraged. The lolita won't pose for him. She won't let him in. She gags when she goes down. She bites. He has had a hard-on for two days.

"I fingered her until my arm was sore up to *here!*" He chops at an elbow. "She was moaning like a banshee, and wouldn't you know it, the *fuck*ing *Vi*king came walking in."

"Why didn't you lock the door?"

"Bitch!"

There is a measure of joy with Bailey. Tobias Paley Gorsham III. He survived, uncircumsized. He is as rare as a whooping crane. It is a beautiful, sexy toy, a well-formed penis with a foreskin. It makes a sense of it all. He talks of the trouble and pain. He would have the tip purple-red, exposed. He has a Jewish doctor. I warn him about that.

I dream of a dangerous woman. She is middle-aged and plump. Her husband rules the tribe. She approaches his tent on a warm spring day; his concubine has birthed a son. She carries a cauldron of soup stirred with the hind leg of a bufotinine-producing toad. Beneath her skirt is concealed a small, sharp knife. She looks like my mother. The tableau freezes.

I awake to a caress between my thighs. I am made love to and come. Fear is a great exciter. Bailey takes me in his arms and kisses the back of my neck. "Sarah, you are *so* good." It speaks of much pleasure. Where has he learned to like women?

N    BEQFNZ   DQ   QRYTXPTW

FTNW SDGG:

D NX QRV N MDGT RA AGEAA ZRE SREGF

GDUT VR BSTTM EQFTW VJT WEO.

BNWNJ

I score. It is not such a hard matter. I take my time driving north through Colorado, picking up hitchhikers. They are plentiful, but the smoke is not.

"Do you have some grass for sale?" I ask.

"No, man. I'm off drugs. I'm into natural foods."

I finally get turned on by a clean-shaven young man with a small knapsack. His jacket is suede and aromatic. He is going to New York to buy. Good. A change of plans. I will drive him there. Colorado is getting cold. I have nothing else to do.

We fall into an easy rap; he spells me at the wheel. We plan to spend the night with friends of his near Omaha who left New York to homestead for a living on land presented free by relatives, but they are crazy with the solitude. We eat and leave. The hitchhiker produces speed and we drive straight through. We hit the Jersey oil-refinery row in late afternoon pink light and haze. WNEW-FM has gone soft, like a teen-age boy adjusting a rubber. We bitch about them.

Secaucus is in our nostrils.

"Sarah?" the hitchhiker says.

"Yes."

"Can I ask you a personal question?"

"Sure."

"Okay. Why are you so fat?"

Good question. "I like fingers grundging around in my cunt and I was too uptight to tell my husband."

It is close enough.

I slap his hand away.

New York is hostile, too complicated. I feel a strange *déjà vu*. I return single breasted to a lover of flesh. We weave our way through the Lower East Side.

We pass a string of stores I know: a Polish butcher

shop, two greengrocers, a dairy store, a bakery, a liquor store.

"I lived there for almost four years," I tell the hitchhiker. "In that building. On the third floor. The man I was married to still lives there. Sweep, his name is. It's a great loft."

"Want to stop?"

"No, sir, I do not."

We end up in a tenement on Fifth Street, near Avenue C. The hall assaults the senses like a she cat in heat. I can feel the bile rising. I rest often and still barely make it. Don't dealers ever live on the first floor?

The hitchhiker's connection is a black dumpling with decayed teeth; his old lady is a white junkie. They give the hitchhiker a warm greeting.

The place is a grand mess. I feel right at home. We make room on the floor near a round table. The Beatles' white album is on the changer. The dumpling produces grass; his old lady is on the nod. The grass comes on slow and then charges up the brain.

"Beautiful smoke, man. Is this what's around?" the hitchhiker says.

"Yeah," the man says. "Gorilla grass."

"I'm up for some quantity."

"Not for a while. Sorry. I'll give you a name."

"How come?"

"Mercury's gone retrograde. I only deal ounces when Mercury's retrograde. Hey, Sarah, what's your sign?"

"Virgo. Near the cusp of Leo."

"Rising sign? Moon?"

"Virgo. Virgo."

"Wow!" he says. "Out of sight."

The junkie dame props an elbow on the cluttered table and focuses laser eyes. "You know something," she says. "I don't make it with fat Virgos. My first husband was a fat Virgo, the stupid mother-fucking bastard." She aims a finger at me. "Bang. Bang," she says.

"Toot-toot." What else is there to say?

She slaps her hand violently on the table and comes up with a squashed roach. She displays it on a flat palm. "Yeah," she says. "Everyone is afraid of getting cut." She rummages in a bag of wool near the table and offers me her works.

It is tempting. She knows a lot. I shake my head and pull on the flesh at my upper arm. "This is enough," I tell her.

I take the hitchhiker to my favorite restaurant in Chinatown. We gorge. Fried dumplings and butterfly shrimps, hot spiced beef, pork with black mushrooms, home-style bean curd, kumquats, candied ginger. The hitchhiker offers me a hundred dollars to drive him back to Colorado with the grass he plans to buy. I decide to go along. I will hie me to the desert yet. The hitchhiker calls and sets up the scoring meeting. He buys dinner. There is a parking ticket on the Porsche. I wad it in a ball and toss it in the gutter.

The address that the hitchhiker has been given is on Eighty-Ninth Street. West. A renovated brownstone. The apartment is on the fourth floor. There is no elevator. The hallway is clean and mirrored. Just what I need. I have eaten too much food. I have felt better in my life.

The dealer's apartment is a shock. It is a museum of dead butterflies and bugs mounted behind glass, of hair wreaths and snake skins. There is a shrunken head hanging from a chandelier, turning slowly round in a hidden draft. It makes my skin crawl.

"Nearly didn't make it up the stairs," I say. I am sliding away. The cold tight knot is upon me. There is a presence about the woman who deals dope from this place. She is like cocaine, a heightener of special senses.

"Really?" she says.

"I know what it is! I've heard about you. You're a friend of Bailey Gorsham's. I remember him mentioning you—on my wedding night, as a matter of fact. He brought us some hash. I'm Sarah Campbell. Bailey and I are old friends. I introduced him to my ex-old man, who's a saxophone player. They wrote some songs together."

"Really?" she says. "That's nice. He's due here any minute."

In the silence the door buzzer shrieks like rasped chalk. I ask for the bathroom and retreat. I wash my face and gargle, urinate and soap my hands, urinate again and feel better. I have caught my breath.

Oh, god. The mistake that I have made by coming here is nearly lethal.

Both Bailey and Sweep are standing in the livingroom. The shrunken head is framed between their heads. The perspective makes me dizzy.


My gun is a Ruger single-six with a .22 Magnum cylinder. I check into a motel as Sarah M. Tabled. There is a comfort in the feebleness of the jest I have not found for quite some time within the center of my drum. I clean the pistol thoroughly, removing the screws with my pocket-knife's screwdriver. It is adequate. I use a little blade to X the lead of a long bullet.

I take a shower. When I am standing I can no longer see my toes. Nor can I when I lie. A fat Virgo. My feet are swollen. My ankles hurt. My thighs. Everything is just out of reach. It is time. Too bad. My boobs have grown large enough at last. I towel dry and insert a Tampax for the hell of it...*it's the only thing I could do half right, and it's turning out all wrong, ma....*

I phantasize a tantrum.

It is twenty miles now to Will's house. I have come very far. I use the Porsche. It is a machine archetypal of what machines should be. I have made a decision. It is a source of power.

There is a clarity to the New England landscape. It is bought at great price. In the light of the moon I pass before my house. Snow is smooth around it, nearly level with the lowest window sills. I have left it behind. It looks deserted.

Will's house is unlit. It is very late. I lean my head back against the seat and hold the Ruger to my temple. No. That will not do. It is a very gory splash I am after. I have got used to the sight of blood; Will has never been to war.

I spin the cylinder of the gun. The noise echoes in a wide, long corridor lined with yellow tile. I stick the barrel in my mouth. It is cold, like the tongue probe of a lover just come.

There is a click, and it is over.

# Chapter Four

And I cannot come to terms with New York, either. I left the hitchhiker waiting on a street corner. He is no worse off than before. I have come to roost in a town named Bronxer, Iowa. I do not know how I got here. I was watching in the rear-view mirror.

It is as good a place as any. I have a sunny room in a boarding house. The bed is brass and creaky. There are white lace curtains on the window, a hand-braided rug, a crocheted antimacassar on the stuffed chair. There is a nice table, just the right size. It is all clean and warm. I have brought three 1,000-piece interlocking jigsaw puzzles. It was too difficult to make a choice.

Meals are served communally. The food is simple, passed along on big white ironstone platters. A woman called Marge shops, does the laundry and cooks; a man called Joe washes the dishes and cleans. I like watching him make up my bed.

I stay until the first day of winter. It is all I can manage. I am embarrassed by the amount of food I am consuming. People would be acquainted with me. I do not have time for that. The people in my head are a full-time

occupation. The puzzles are done. I leave Bronxer, Iowa in
the middle of the afternoon, walking out on the bill.

Will goes to California for two weeks to visit his
parents. The lolita gives her precious hymen to the leader
of the local high school gang, which numbers four. When
Will returns, she still won't let him in. He decides that
makes her something special. I do not see the logic.
Young Viking cracks up his car and breaks a big toe.
Sam the guitar maker catches me pissing in the sink.
Better him than my local.

I register in a motel as Holly Woodlawn. Why not? We
are both impersonators of women. It is mid-afternoon. I
have brought a tub of Colonel Sanders' Recipe Golden
Fried Chicken, a bag of candy corn left from Hallowe'en, a
bottle of Asti Spumante. I put it to chill in the blue-
speckled styrofoam ice bucket with the white lid. Whoopie!
Tonight will be New Year's Eve.
In the next room, a couple is already making it.

Ernest lands an order for 500 assorted pieces of pottery
from a New York store and throws a party. He and Bridie
are in hock to the Boston hospital. They serve $2.00 the
half-gallon cheap-o white wine, in beautiful salt-glazed
stoneware mugs. There is grass from a dynamite closet
crop.
Will has brought the lolita. I do not envy him. He is in
rut for her. She is wearing pink hot pants with tiny silver
buckles at the sides and waist.
The Broadmans have been having plumbing trouble.
Hargrove has been invited with his wife. I meet her for the
first time. She is buxom and gushes. Hargrove heads for the
wine.
Young Viking is home, nursing his broken toe.
Sam spends the evening with Bridie's college room-
mate, who is visiting from Little Rock.
Sandra arrives with a very presentable man. Where has

she found him? It is as surprising as the ball-bearinged eyes on Will's Linus Pauling sculpture, which is finally completed. I have been haunted by it for two days. Will has motorized the eyes and they revolve. He has modeled the head and features after Richard Avedon's photograph. I should have brought the sculpture with me as an escort. It would have been appropriate. The party is a horror show worthy of *Nothing Personal*.

"Hey, Sarah. You've put on another five pounds." It is Will, of course. He is right. July is going to be a good month. I weighed in this morning at 145. He is drunk, his eyes small and mean. Lolita stands silently a step behind and tightens the buckle at her right thigh. She is, after all, a pretty little thing.

"I've stopped smoking tobacco. I was strip-mining my lungs."

"Better watch it. At your age cancer's better than a double chin."

"Fuck off, mister."

"Watch your language, sweetheart, there's a lady present." He takes the lolita's hand and moves her beside him.

"Cool it, folks." Ernest to the rescue with some smoke. He puts an arm around Will's shoulder and offers him the joint first.

"You're both pigs."

"Hey, hey," Will says. "Name calling is against the rules."

"How about swine? Does that make it?"

"No, ma'am," Ernest says.

"What is this, a gang-bang?"

"Language, language!" Will retrieves his hand and tisks his fingers like a peeler attacking a carrot.

"Put your hands in your pockets, Will. Maybe they can find a little something to play with."

"Score one," Ernest says. I guess I know the game.

Will holds a hand to his chest. "You are talking, to paraphrase Norman Mailer, about the median Methodist member we both know and love. Your remark, madam—"

"I'm not a madam."

"Your remark, madam," Will continues, "was below the belt."

"Did you know word playing is an early symptom of schizophrenia?" I address myself to the lolita. Her brow is annoying me. It is smooth, like veal from the leg of milk-fed calf. "Did you know it's catching? Like incipient poverty of manners? Will has them both, my dear. Poor girl, and with the golden opportunities of high school still before you." Ouch.

"Ouch," Ernest says.

If it's good enough for him, I'll take it. Two points. It's better than nothing. I am the party's extra female, a useless thing. For this I moved out of the City?

The fucking ooze is back. I barely believe it. I find a gynecologist in Lincoln, Nebraska. His window faces the State Capitol Building tower, which looks like an enormous golden prick.

I weigh in at 197 pounds.

"Don't you think it's about time to go on a diet?" the doctor says.

"No," I tell him. "I'm aiming for two fifty."

"Why?" he asks, his voice nicely incredulous.

"It's a good round figure."

He prescribes pills for the vaginitis and hopefully produces a mimeographed diet form.

I wad it in a ball and litter the street.

I am right on schedule. I return to Bronxer, Iowa at high noon. The debt is costing me my peace of mind.

They make it mighty easy. Joe of the straightening rumpled sheets squinches his mouth and peers over rimless glasses and Marge of the onion hands elaborately totals up my bill with a genuine pencil stub.

As if they didn't know it to the penny.

May they cluck their tongues for many a year.

Bronxer, Iowa? *ZAP—you're a nightmare...toot-toot.*

*January 15, 1972*

*Dear Sweep:*

*I have been crossing things off my list of things to do in this new year, and your letter of August 21 is next. I realize that I could have given you my decision when we met last month, but the surprise of seeing you and Bailey quite pushed it out of my mind. I thought your comment that I had "acquired some insulation" was quite funny, by the way, even if I did not respond well at the time.*

*In any event, as your lawyer has certainly told you, we have been in touch by mail and phone. It seems to me that my end of this business is now in order, at least legally, with the exception of the matter of the drum. This letter is to advise you that I am not now or at any other time going to part with the drum. It is absolutely true, as you state in your letter, that Will handed the drum directly to you, but it was certainly offered as a house gift and as such falls into the category of personal effects. Under the terms of the agreement drafted by your lawyer, such effects are to be divided by mutual consent, and I do not consent. Further, I did not ask for any of the items you list as having given to me. They are "Given to Sarah" only because they are still in the house. You left the furniture pieces behind to avoid paying a mover, and the rest of the stuff you didn't want. I could make a similar list of things I left behind at the loft, but I've lived without them now for a long time, and have learned that I don't need them. In the end, I think it balances out. With the exception of the drum, you will be welcome to come and take any of the other things on your list at some point in the* future, although I do not know when I will be returning to New England.

I have been travelling since the summer, up and down and across the country. I have finally gotten to see some of the places you used to talk about—Out West—and I am heading back towards Arizona by a roundabout route, taking my time. I am going to drive further south than I did before. I am anticipating a place where it will be warm— perhaps I will even go to Mexico!—because despite my "insulation" I am, as usual, cold, although not as cold as I was last winter when you took that four-night-a-week gig in the city and I was in the house alone with the chunk stove.

But in any event, it is another year, and just now I am in a drafty room in a once-private house that takes in overnight guests. I have taken to stopping in such houses occasionally instead of a motel if I spot one that looks interesting. This one is owned and run by a couple in their late sixties, and they have a set speech about the place. They have "retained the first floor of the house" for their own use, although the down- stairs livingroom, which juts out to the back, "is sometimes used communally at night. There is a large stone and mortar fireplace, which was built in 'twenty-one by the missus' grandfather when he added the room to the original dwelling, which was built in eighteen seventy-nine." Isn't that interesting?

I always did want to ask you why you didn't buy me a sweater for Christmas instead of doing what you did, but I guess I got around to playing the drum instead.

Hope this finds you well.

                                        Sarah

Viking has made his recovery. He doesn't even need a cane.
He wants to compare bone breaks. I can't help him out. He
has installed a No-Pest Strip above his bed. I lay the
*Ramparts* ecology rap on him. No sale.

Young Viking has not replaced his car. He insists on
driving if we take the Porsche. He doesn't like riding with a
female behind the wheel. We are to go meet with a couple
of his friends. They have some grass for sale. He is from a
small industrial city about 70 miles to the southeast. We
split half a dose of sunshine acid.

Hitchhiking is easy if you know where you're going.
You stand on the road, hold out a thumb and a car stops. It
is a magnificent summer day. We conquer the landscape
like Harold in Italy. The car lets us out beneath a viaduct
overpass. We scramble up a path worn in the grass and
change levels.

Four rides and ninety minutes later we enter Sam's
Pizza Parlour, Inc. There are three couples in booths, two
braless girls in T-shirts and tight pants dancing to Neil
Young on the jukebox in an alcove near the door, three
guys in army jackets at a table in the middle of the floor.
They are trying not to watch the girls.

"We're early," Young Viking says. "We made good
time." He pats me on the rump. "It helps to hitch with a
good-looking chick."

"Thank you, sir," I say. "You've made my day."

"Where the hell have you been?" Will says. "I thought
we had a date."

"What the hell are you doing in my bed?"

Will is in an expansive mood; he pontificates.

"Man is a taker," he says, "woman a giver."

"I'm not so sure of that."

The smell of my cunt is on his fingers. He knows I
didn't come. He passes his hand lightly across my upper
lip, as if I need the reminder, before tweaking at my left
nipple.

He says, "Woman is the provider of sustenance, that means she's a giver."

"So how's the lolita these days?" I say.

"God, you're a bitch, Sarah."

"Bitches do great, they've got a lot of tits. The more tits, the more sustenance, right?"

"Opinionated, too. Why don't you just listen to me for once."

"Look, I heard you. Provider of sustenance. By which you meant I've got the milk bottles and for some reason you think that makes you allowed to take. It's not true, Will."

"You're just like every other stupid cunt, aren't you? You reduce everything to 'it isn't fair.'"

"I didn't say 'it isn't fair,' and what's a stupid cunt, anyway?"

"What is a whore?" He reaches down and probes.

I would have sold myself not to have moaned.

"I am a whore."

Bobby Fischer, where are you?


Will throws a celebration barbecue. He has had a letter published in *The New York Times* about the art and joy of growing radishes. El Bridie is nowhere in sight. Ernest and I leave the others to go play a little clit twiddle in the studio. We drink bourbon from the bottle. Too bad, sister.

It is dusk when we return. Will begins a round of applause. I curtsy and lift my skirt to the knee. Ernest is very drunk and staggers. The Bridie backs to the fringe, her face pale. How easy it is to stare her down.


I am concerned about structure, the patterns of my life. I have indigestion. Is it the large economy size Hershey bar I have just eaten, or a remnant of my past stuck in the gut? My disguise is admirable. I have outfitted myself in a Stout Shop. I am a perfect size 22½—45, 39, 48. I register in a motel as Phillis C. Horney.

And the demon is upon me. The unravelings at the

edge. The musty smell of the hot attic room and cracker crumbs on a sheet.

I roll a joint.

I crack open the bottle of gin instead.

Better tears than pain.

He was a man in his fifties anyway, and badly married.

It is 2 a.m. I can not sleep. There is an all-night hamburger joint next to the motel and the fuchsia neon sign winks are driving me crazy.

At one table, eyes downcast, is a large woman. She is heavier than me, I think, but neatly dressed. She has an ugly 3-hair mole on one cheek and a bad moustache made worse with pink face powder. She has no lines on her face, none at all, and pendulous earlobes that round out from within at the bottom.

She is blushing with discomfort.

Lounging in the aisle near her table, looking down, stand three goons in black leathers. The jackets read: HEAVEN'S DEVILS and below, embroidered in cerise, *We were born to eat pussy.*

"Hey, look at that!"

They turn to look at me.

"What is this, a fatso convention?" one says.

"A double burger, french fries, and a large coke, please."

The girl behind the counter is whistling to herself in short breaths, fussing with make-work. She looks up to take my order. Against her will—I can see the battle—her eyes dart to the aisle, searching out the pussy eaters.

"It'll be a minute," she says. "Their order is first."

"Sure."

"Damn right sure, fatso." It is the smallest of the three. He is also the dirtiest, and has a wicked burn scar on the side of his neck. He wears a heavy gold earring. He rocks on his heels, then saunters in our direction.

His sidekicks fall into formation behind.

He brushes me aside, leans on the counter and begins

emptying a paper napkin dispenser, one by one, onto the floor.

"Getting hungry," he says to the girl. "Ain't that right, boys?"

"Yeah."

"Yeah."

"Almost ready, sir," the girl says.

"Good."

My food comes first, pushed through a slot from the kitchen on a tray.

"Hey, what gives?"

"Yeah!"

"Yours is being wrapped for take-out, sir," the girl says. "It takes just a wee bit longer."

The fat woman pushes up from her booth and leaves. I sit at a table to eat. In a minute the girl carries three bags to the counter.

The leader grins, reaches out and seizes the girl by the arm.

"Okay. Let's go chick. Grab the food and your coat."

"Please," she whimpers, "don't hurt me. Here are your Whopper Burgers." She holds out the bags.

I can not help it. My laughter wrenches free and is beyond my control.

"Hey, what's with her?" The girl's arm is released and she flees to the kitchen.

"Don't know, Ponzo," one of the sidekicks says.

"Hey, fatso, what's with you?" he yells.

I shake my head, unable to speak.

"Hey, maybe she's crazy."

"Yeah."

"Yeah!"

Yeah, yeah, yeah....

They depart with a great roar of motorcycle noise. It is January, and I am nearly back to the Rocky Mountains. I admire their fortitude.

The kitchen door opens.

The counter girl comes to my table.

"Thank you." She hands me a Roast Beef Special.
"This is for you. You were great. Weren't they *terrible*. You
saved my life I think, yes, you really did."

It brings violin strains to my head. "And I'd like you to
know, my dear," I say, "that your long search is ended. *I* am
your real mother."

# Chapter Five

Once, I wanted to be beautiful. I have had the feeling. It is very nice. Surely there is something else that matters.

Forgive me.

It is raining, and very grim. I am homesick. The sound of rain on snow is the sound of rain on snow. I would secure my memories in a dark cedar chest and fasten the lid with a Gordian knot. Oh, Lord, what am I to do? I have lost sight of my place. The world outside the dirty window waits. I have pulled up the Venetian blind. It took nearly all my energy.

The grossness of my image fills the mood. I sit in an armchair and prepare to watch the Monday traffic cruising by. The motel abuts a black macadam road. Come on, now, road, show me some stuff!

The sound of tires throwing slush means spring is sure to come.

I inspect the situation. My legs are very hairy. I cross one up and confront the foot. It is mottled, and the nails are yellow, thick and ridged. Eureka, I've got leprosy. Or at least the gout. And there is a terrible rough redness to the skin of the thigh.

Good.

I'll call the matter settled.

No beach this year, Sarah my girl.

"So you finally got in."
Will is at my door, grinning. "Yup," he says. "Got any beer?"
"Sure."
He gives me the blow-by-blow. It is more than I care to hear.
"It was a good thing we were down by the lake," he concludes. "Any time we wanted to we could go in for a dip. That's the best way to make it with a cunt who's on the rag."
I must remember not to drink beer at 8 a.m. It makes for a sour stomach.
"Hey, Will. When did she become a cunt?"
"What do you mean?"
"She was a lady at Ernest's party."

Sandra is in love. He is the young man from the party. His name is Hank. He is an ex-Seminary student, a draft resister, returned home to face the town.
She arrives late on a Wednesday evening, direct from her lib meeting.
"I was taught to believe in marriage," she says. "That my virginity means something. It's as if my whole structure is being threatened. I think they meant well, but I asked for support because I'm very confused and they came at me like a wrecking crew." She begins to cry.
"Are you getting any sleep, Sandra?"
"No, not much."
I get her into a warm bath and tuck her into the guestroom.
In the morning she is gone. There are clean sheets on the bed and a thank-you note pinned to the pillow. She has washed and put away a week's worth of dirty dishes. Let's hear it for the Salvation Army, folks.

"You are an incredible horny broad," Bailey says.

"Yeah?"

"Yeah," he says.

"Are there any more of them like you at home?"

"Nope. Just me," he says.

"Good. That's all I can handle. Come on. Take me for a walk to the lake."

We are to go watch the horse pulls at the annual county fair. The heat creates a dilemma. I am definitely getting fat. I cover the worst of it with a knee-length gypsy skirt and tuck a long red halter top inside the wide elastic waistband. Safer than shorts.

It is 2:35 when they come. Will has the ribbon for his blue-prize winning cabbage pinned to the left pocket of a workshirt. He is prouder of that than of any of his sculptures. We sit three abreast in the cab of his pick-up. I get the middle.

We are guided into a parking row by a series of cops. I am surprised by the number of vehicles.

Young Viking has brought a bottle of Seagram's disguised as a brown paperbag. Will has a six-pack and a couple extra Budweisers. We decide to hit the booze. The air is stifling. Beneath the skirt my thighs and stomach sweat. Toot-toot. I will have prickly heat.

"Where to?" I say. "I want out of this Turkish bath."

"The horse pulls are this-a-way," Will says. He leaps out the driver's door. "County Fair, we are *here!*" he yells, throwing his arms wide. A beer bottle escapes his bag and explodes against a well-placed rock.

"Come on, Sarah. You're not going to believe the horse pulls either." Young Viking takes my arm and we slide out of the truck.

I am possessed with an urgency I do not understand. I am beside my mother in a room of white smells, pressing a moistened towel to her mouth. I can not help her thirst. I am nineteen. I retreat with the visiting hour, although I could have stayed, to masturbate until some faceless caller claims the night for death.

How is it possible to endure? My demons are clamoring for release. They do battle in the tension zones. There is a threat above my eyes; another deep inside the middle of my chest. I lift my sagging breasts. There are brown spots around the nipples. When did they stop being freckles?

I check out an armpit. When all else fails, try a long hot soothing bath. Advice from *Cosmopolitan*. Do they know about motel living? One can leave the grundge ring behind.

I am definitely involved in a headache.

I approach my first county fair. I walk behind Will and Young Viking. We have separated to pass a short, sweaty man, beer-bellied, with his family: twin daughters eating cotton candy, a pre-adolescent son with a caramel apple, an overweight wife in bright yellow slacks with thick horizontal stripes. The stripes are hunter green.

There are strong smells—Italian sausage, onions, charcoal-grilled chicken....Has my deodorant stopped working?

"Sam!" Will yells.

I spot the guitar maker ahead. He turns around and waits for us to catch up. He has Ernest's Bridie by the arm. She is wearing Bermuda shorts and has dirty smudges on her calves.

"Hey, man, have you ever seen anything like this?" Will extends his cabbage's blue ribbon with a thumb.

Sam produces a tape measure and takes it to the ribbon. "Nope," he says. "Never have."

There is a good laugh. A sudden enthusiasm. We head en masse for the sporting event arenas at the far end of the fair. The aisles are a sea of mud. Walkways have been created with wooden planks. I will have mud splotches on the backs of my legs.

We have spent the afternoon at the horse pulls, drinking rye with beer chasers.

Young Viking makes his move for the toilet. "Off to
see a man," he says.

The next-to-the-last weight class of horses has finished
competition. There is an intermission. It is nearly six-
thirty. I am attacked by a hunger and mosquitoes are doing
damage to my arms. I go scouting for a hot sausage grinder
and insect repellent.

There is a happening near the midway. Two women
gyrate on a raised platform before a tent; a hard-sell barker
hawks tickets. Do they need to fuck him to keep their jobs?

The overripe Italian wears a black corselet, laced up
the front. She cups unmanageable breasts in her hands. On
each side of her tightly costumed crotch, dark pubic hair
escapes.

The blonde is covered by a long-sleeved grey dress with
a high white collar. She moves in small steps and holds the
mid-thigh length skirt to the top of her long black
stockings, exposing the garters, which are red, with three
fingers of each hand, the pinkies extended in graceful
curves. She is flirting with a pair of soldiers below her to
the left. Has she remembered or learned the blush?


I replace the can of insect repellent in the glove
compartment of Will's pick-up and thread my way back
toward the sporting event arenas at the far end of the plank
runways.

Tired children are acting up. A small boy empties his
stomach into a garbage can, helped up to its edge by his
mother. There are three other children with her. They are
all under ten. She must really look forward to the annual
county fair.

The crowd begins to thicken. The horse pulls must be
over. I leave the planks and cut to the other side of the
midway.

Three women now gyrate on the raised platform before
the tent. There is a major attraction in the middle, a young
woman with gorgeous long platinum-blonde hair. Did I
see her mingling with her audience in the afternoon?

Slowly, arms above her head, she bumps and grinds in her
full-length black plunging-neckline Harlow dress.

Her armpits are shaved.

How has the barker got her hooked? Does he keep her
waiting for it days at a time?

I spot Will. He is on the far side of the crowd with
Sam, Ernest's Bridie and the lolita. Where has she come
from? She is wearing red hot pants and a bikini top. Is she
really less than half my age?

I buy a SMILE button from a roaming vendor and head
over.

"Howdy, folks."

"Well, look who's here," the lolita says. Her hand rests
on the cabbage's blue ribbon pinned to Will's shirt. She
graces him with a sultry pout. Has she designs on the
dancing girl's job?

"Where's Young Viking?" I ask.

"Still in the can, I think," Sam says.

"What's he doing, getting blown in there?"

Bridie colors nicely.

"Where's Ernest?" I ask her.

"Home working." She avoids my eyes and searches the
crowd. Is she looking to get really fucked? The predatory
single men, in pairs and small packs, have slunk in with
the dusk.

Standing alone behind me, wearing mirrored sunglasses, is a large meaty man with a small almost bald head.
He is motionless; his face is flushed. His flowered shirt is
tucked into a pair of belted ochre slacks that constrain his
middle like a string between fat 1-pound liverwursts. He is
very light of skin and has sunburned in blotches on the
back of his neck, his nose and high forehead. He is
watching the Italian girl jiggle her boobs. He licks the
corners of his open mouth with a delicatessen tongue.

I get it.

We are all part of the show.


I make a move.

It is Tuesday.

The roads are clear.

I head south through the Rockies, toward desert country.

I smoke a joint.

I have a reverie.

Everyone out there knows I have sex organs!

What am I going to do about that?

I test the speed limits and the local cops.

There is an 8-thousand foot high plateau ahead.

The Porsche delivers.

The head of my drum has warmed up at last. From deep within its center it talks back to my hands. I approach a low rumble from a middle tone, holding back too much, and the swell disassembles in an irregular beat. Is it mocking me? I slow down to listen, but it changes tone. I play around with the 12-beat pattern and finally reachieve the power loss. Irregularity has its uses. I would learn what it has to say.

"I'm horny," I say.

"In order to make it I need an erection between my legs."

"So?"

Lips and Hayworth return. Lips is driving the green Pontiac convertible. I have a moment and invite them in for a cup of coffee.

It is wonderful. They are very dedicated and will not yield even in the face of small talk. They are sisters.

"Where are you from?" I ask Hayworth.

"Lincoln, Nebraska," she says. "The state's capitol. Nebraskans are proud of their capitol building and its splendid golden tower, which is in the shape of an upright ear of corn."

"How long have you lived in New England?" I ask Lips.

"Eleven years this December," she says. "Did you know that in Proverbs, verse eleven, line twenty-five, it is said: 'He that withholdeth corn, the people shall curse him: but blessing shall be—' "

"Verse eleven, line twenty-*six*," Hayworth says.

"...but blessing shall be upon the head of him that selleth it," Lips says.

The local is the way I like him, wide-eyed and dazzled and silent. I am in an expansive mood and pontificate.

"The thing about getting high," I tell him, "is that the possibilities for experience are limitless. More feelings, stronger feelings, a larger center."

The local doesn't move. I am playing with his cock. I offer him the joint. He refuses.

I put his hand between my legs and hold it there. It is much more reluctant than my own. I release the pressure and his arm falls to the bed.

Okay. I let go of him and offer a 3-second preview.

"You do *that!*" He sits up abruptly.

"Sure."

"My wife and...you know—"

"Yeah, your true love."

"They don't do that."

"I'm willing to bet that one or both of them is lying."

"Do it," he says.

There is a crisis in the clan. Bridie is caught making it with Sam. Ernest throws her out of the house. Do you believe it?

I go to keep him company. He is planning a series of ashtrays to be called "Men of Courage." He is making sketches of distended scrotums and long flaccid penises to send to the New York store.

"Shit. You sure make it hard for yourself," I say.

"I don't give a damn," he says. "She's a rotten bitch. No broad's ever done that to me before."

"What?"

"Gone screwing on the side. And I *married* her."

"You haven't exactly been faithful to her," I reminded him.

"Okay. So it isn't fair. Fuck it. I've got the weight of history on my side."


Will had supplied a bottle of Retsina. We were in his bed. He was in a generous mood. He should have been; I had let him use the back of my throat.

"What do you want, Sarah?" he asked. "Is there something you'd like me to do?"

I performed an act of courage.

I found and told the truth.

No one said it was going to be easy.

"I need to come too," I said. "It's my turn, Will."

There was no movement.

"I'd really rather not," he said. "You just got over your period a couple of days ago. Do you mind very much?"

"Oh, no. I enjoy being frustrated."

"Don't get nasty."

"I wasn't being nasty. You asked what I wanted and I told you."

"That's out. I don't really like to do it anyway. It's too small and hard to find."

"Oh, Christ, what do you want me to do? Thank you for telling me the truth or apologize for the way my body is made?"

"No, you don't have to do either. Just stop turning me off, that's all."


My head is on Bailey's shoulder. He toys with my hair. We have had a good one in the dry heat of a Saturday afternoon.

"What do you want to do with your life?" he asks me.

We are in the small room under the attic eaves. I am too slow to catch the mosquito buzzing around my head.

"I'll settle for fucking it away," I say.

It is good for a laugh.

The joke is on me.

I cut the time off from both ends of my life. It cannot be helped. How can I deal with the laughter when it strains the muscles of my heart? My mortality offends me. Regrets cause hardening of the arteries.

I know where I'm at at last. It is nearly noon, although I can not see the sun. The month is March. My pulse rate is 120. I weigh 216 pounds. I walk along a dirt road in a freaky southern Arizona blizzard. The Porsche has run out of gas. See. It is very simple.

I am having a delusion of grandeur. It is the year 2958. A class of anthropology students is gathered at a spot a hundred meters ahead.

"We stand here today," a young woman professor is saying, "before the wonderful ice-preserved *Sarah,* the justly famed example of pre-neo-rationalistic weight...."

# PART II

*You say I am repeating*
*Something I have said before. I shall say it again.*
— T. S. Eliot, *The Four Quartets*

# Chapter One

It is full moon. Ye olde golden scapegoat is window framed in a remarkable starry sky. It must be nearly midnight. Witch riding clouds in wispy layers scoot by now and again. The wind is playing high. It is still here near the ground. The mattress platform on which I lie is relatively comfortable. The quilt provided is generous in size. The Volkswagen camper is reasonably warm.

I know what I've done. I've sent a father-to-be named Benjamin and a woman in labor named Chestnut off to find a hospital because I sure am no midwife.

But what the fuck am I doing here?

I have never been on a road the likes of this before. I hope they take it easy with the Porsche. At less than fifteen miles an hour speed it sounded like it felt, as if the pile of metal that surrounded me was being shaken off by sheer brute force.

What did Sweep call it? Those parallel ruts of hard-packed dirt, a standard featured landmark of the roads out here where he grew up?

It begins with a C.

I have a terrible memory.

"It's the melting snow that does it," Sweep said. "The water gets into cracks during the day in the spring, or if there's a thaw in the winter, and freezes up again at night, creating furrows on the dirt roads so that it feels as if you're driving on a washboard. That's what it looks like, also. Water is altogether quirky stuff, you know. It's a solvent and a cleanser and a means of transport and a standard for weights and measures, and if you boil it it turns into something else and when it freezes it expands to become a substance lighter than itself. It's the only liquid which does that. You can use that piece of information in the winter to split huge logs without an axe. You pour water into a crack in the felled trunk and when it freezes the ice forces the crack to expand. Fill it again and it expands some more and eventually you'll split it. Water is t-o-o much."

Corrugation, that's it.

Is it worth it, getting angry at the fates? I rather think it's not. Energy is hard to come by. So what if I'm stuck in a stranger's vehicle tilted useless in a ditch? It is late and I am tired. The problem can wait until morning. I have earned my sleep tonight.

A high thin whine is coming from the moon. A jet plane flying sleeping people to a change. Is it going north or south? Who knows. Perhaps that is a vital piece of information. It is just the kind of problem that I like to solve to help get me through a difficult night. When daylight comes I can write the question on a piece of paper. Stuff it in a helium-filled balloon. Send it out into the world. If I had some helium and a balloon.

I think I'm going crazy.

It really is too good to be true.

An encounter in the middle of nowhere on a nameless corrugated road. It must have been two hours ago, say ten o'clock at night. Enter, in the eerie light of a full moon, one fat woman driving slower than a four-ton caterpillar, with her car headlights off, no less, because queer shadow shapes were living on the surface of a vast surrealist landscape, and a young man in a plaid lumberjacket standing nonchalantly next to the left rear fender of a battered blue Volkswagen camper which is obviously disabled. It is angled off the right side of the road, the victim of a low shoulder.

He waves her down; she brakes to a stop.

He, who turns out to be tall, thin and bearded, approaches; she lowers the window of a cluttered two-seater 1965 red Porsche.

"You're not going to believe this," she says, telling the truth, "but this morning I ran out of gas a hundred miles north in a snowstorm and now I'm looking for a place to spend the night. Some joker sent me off on this thing some people call a road. Miserable clown. I hope he rots in solitude in a rat-filled tenement basement. If I ever reach a destination, I'm going to get me a map."

"Chestnut's having the baby. She's in the back of the camper. Can you help?"

Perhaps I should recall it straight from the beginning. But I can not. I certainly have lost control. No memories predate the age of six. I suspect there may have been some happy feelings in those blocked out early years. I would like to think that, so I do.

I was shown photographs of the tall good-looking man who, it is said, married my mother and was responsible for my birth. I am told that he was proud of me. I can not, of course, imagine that. Pride. The conception. Once, at the age of eleven, just before she remarried, I surprised my mother coming from her room. She was wearing nothing but a half slip and a lacy bra across her bosom. I never heard her say the word breasts. Perhaps the 'sts' sound was too difficult for her tongue to master. That was the closest that I ever came to seeing the whole body of my mother, although once, in my early teens, soon after she lost the baby, I bathed her feet when bursitis in a shoulder made it difficult for her to shower.

I had a first-grade teacher named Miss Warbler. She had deep lines around her eyes. She wore her faded dull brown hair in braids across the top of her head. She had a dress with red goldfish that swam across her broad back when she wrote on the blackboard. She wore the dress on Thursday.

On Wednesday there was chocolate cookies with the milk.

On Tuesday and Friday we had science in the afternoon.

"What if water didn't freeze?" Miss Warbler asked. "Why, if water didn't freeze, there would be no ice. If there were no ice, there would be so much water in the oceans that everything would be flooded and there would be no place for people to live. So you see, boys and girls, water is very important."

The Chinese know how to make a treat of it.

Split the neck of a fattened cow and watch the blood run out. Avoid the kicking of the legs. You need a hunk of fresh raw meat, preferably from the rump, to pass through the finest blades of a meat grinder. Knead a bit of rice wine, soy and cornstarch into the ground beef with the hands, just to get the feel of it.

Shuck some oysters from the privacy of their shells with a sharp pointed knife and smoke them alive, then drown to make sure in salted oil of cotton seed until they turn a smooth rich oaken brown with just a tinge of the green the mind associates with bile. Chop well beneath the whetstoned razor edge of a thick-handled cleaver.

You will need a wok and fresh green peas for contrast, texture, color, shape. There are, of course, alternatives. Aren't there always alternatives? Celery stalks, sliced quite thin, for instance.

But it isn't quite the same.

Prepare the wok, anoint and offer to high heat.

Let thirty seconds pass, then add the beef. It will forget the color of its blood while writhing in the oil. Drop in the peas when metamorphosis has taken place. Stir to keep the patterns changing. The eye must not get bored.

You must be fast now—a bit of oyster sauce (although hoisin will do) and then the oily bits of mollusk.

Perfectionists will add a small amount of cornstarch mixed with liquid which will put a gleam, a polish if you will, into *every* nook and cranny.

Serve hot on rice or wrapped in lettuce leaves.

I should cook it as a test for lovers.

It smells and tastes of pussy.


"Why do you complicate everything, Sarah?" It is a man's voice I hear talking. "I like things simple." Is he standing by my chair?

"What do you mean, simple?"

"You know. Simple. Easy. Tension free. Uncomplicated."

"Meaning you like things the way they are," I say. It is not a question.

"No. I don't mean that. I simply mean I like things simple. See. You're doing it again."


I must have drifted off. I've got to take a leak but cannot move. It is reassuring to know that my body is still here with the rest of me. It is going to be a long night. Half-formed dreams and anecdotes and situations never understood come floating up like protein scum that fouls a well-earned bath.

The moon has moved perhaps an hour to my right. I can not remember if it's heading east or west, although I care a bit for astronomical information. The names of stars and such. Intimations of infinity. The concept of a light year. That Dante modified and used the astrological conception of causation to find a satisfactory meaning in his view of Christian philosophy. That some Russian peasant woman holds a record with her in the grave for producing 69 red squally babies from the sperm injected into her.

Chestnut. Now that's a moniker to reckon with. I wonder how she came upon it. Did some lover give it to her as a gift? Bailey sometimes calls me Mouse in bed. I like that very much. It identifies with near to certainty that his feelings at the time are warm and pleasingly affectionate. I wonder if his other women feel the same.

There was a bit of trouble with the vehicle exchange. Chestnut's labor pains were still irregular, her water bag intact. I angled the Porsche as best I could to give us light, although the moonlight was quite bright.

I waited beside the man in the plaid jacket, who introduced himself as Benjamin, while Chestnut steadied herself in the side doorway of the camper with a hand on the back of the passenger seat. I have not often looked at a woman if there is a man around. There was a calmness to her bearing. She had a thinnish horsy face, small trapped eyes, large protruding lips, and corkscrew frizzy long black hair, although perhaps she is a pretty woman and the Porsche lights were unkind. She was wearing a tent-shaped dress made from an Indian magenta, brown and orange paisley printed bedspread beneath a light-weight coat.

She lowered herself to sit on the edge of the doorway and let her feet slide down the little incline, reaching for the solid ground. I thought she moved quite agilely until quite suddenly she wrapped her arms around herself. I found it hard to look at that. Women in labor are much too scary.

In the end she needed Benjamin to get her settled in the Porsche, and I accepted help to get me in the side door of the camper. It is an awkward step across the ditch. It took much shifting of my weight and the impetus of desperation.

There was a cat fight outside the window of my house a few weeks after Sweep and I moved in. I suppose that means that I am making progress. I did not think of it as 'my house' then, although it was my money that Sweep and I used for the down payment. My mother's money. The money that my mother left to me. I have squandered more than half the money that my mother left to me.

The house—My house has seven rooms. It is painted

grey with yellow trim and it sits upon a knoll. The southern slope of the knoll, which descends in two decreasing humps to the northern end of a postcard lake a quarter mile away, a part of which is owned by the town, is cut by a county road which meanders to the right, then doglegs left, then right again, across old railroad tracks, before connecting with the main road leading into town. The road forms one boundary of the 15 acres of my land. I considered this southern exposure when I decided to continue making mortgage payments on my house. Sweep's lawyer sounded quite agreeable when we discussed the issue on the telephone.

The slightly larger tom was absolutely white. He had been coming around for days. He left a lot of smell behind him. I did not like him very much. Cats are not at their best for me in white.

The rival had the markings of a tiger on a long-haired coat of brownish silver grey.

The female came from down the road. Her name was Abilene. She was young for her first heat. Black, with amber eyes. There was white on her chest in the shape of a shield and she had elegant white whiskers.

She was dainty as she meowed one small protest and licked her cunt, although perhaps the meow was no protest at all. I doubt if she had expectations worrying her.

The toms turned proper gentlemen, as if by mutual consent, and allowed a modicum of privacy for the toilette. They retreated nearly out of sight, to sit four tail lengths from each other at the edge of a bed of tiger lilies to the left of the attached garage. Sweep said that weathered barn-board structure was a shed. We kept the cars in it. I called it a garage.

It was the suddenness that shocked. Great unexpected tufts of long white hair. Two silhouettes of Hallowe'en. Horrific heaving shrieks, like those of radio commercials for a drive-in horror film.

Abilene walked calmly out of sight.

She seemed quite unconcerned with the responsibility.

It was the tiger cat who slunk away, although I thought the white tom had the worst of it, but I had judged him superficially and on the basis of his excess hair. He ignored the cut above one eye. He flicked an ear. He assumed the pose of a Chinese Foo dog sculpture.

Slowly, head high, Ms. Abilene came mincing back into view. She paraded on a bit before the tom, took good care to angle so the line of vision was quite clear, then flopped to lick and hiss again.

The mating was as short and violent as the fight.

I am in pain. My center has fallen away. I grow small within myself. I am in a dim-lit cave that writhes and groans of its own accord. It is open to the front—am I in an islet of Langerhans?—and the surface is smooth to the touch and the colors of Bryce Canyon.

I can see a small plank platform beyond the mouth; it appears to be floating in space.

I attain the edge.

Across a tree-lined chasm is a vast room built on stilts. The room has a ceiling, a floor and three walls, and retreats from openness into its corners as in an Edward Gorey drawing.

The room is very clean.

Two soft armchairs upholstered in pale green velvet flank a side table. There is a rocking chair, too, and a long sofa.

In the middle of the room is an oblong table, of wooden planks like the platform, which I now see provides a passageway across the chasm by means of a complicated arrangement of horizontal ropes and pulleys. The table is set for dinner, with white cloth napkins and holiday china. There are chairs at the table, and one of them is empty. The people sit rigid in their places, and do not talk. There is an air of expectancy.

Do they wait for me?

I approach the platform, but it will not yet do. It is snarled beyond my reach. I retrieve a rope and begin to free the line, rolling it up as I go, much as winding yarn. But when I stop for a second to rest my hands, or even to blink my eyes, a second line plays out and tangles at my feet.

It is a worry.

It will take much time.

I am in a rush now, for I am cold and very tiny.

They sit in their huge chairs scalped.

I must know if I have been there.

It is like a nightmare.


I have identified the problem.

It is very simple.

I am hungry and my feet are freezing.

I have kicked the sheet and quilt free of their mooring at the bottom of the mattress platform. The camper truck has lost its warmth to the middle of the night. I perform the requisite maneuver and get the bedding tucked beneath my ankles.

Outside the window, beyond the big dipper and the milky way, a constellation I think is Taurus shows six stars and Draco hangs its tail.

The moon continues.

I continue.

You continue.

He, she and it....

# Chapter Two

There is a rhythm to this night I do not like, a pulse and flow peculiar to a kind of dreamy state that comes, I think, from isolation.

No doubt about it.

I am certainly alone.

There are no names I know of for the silent nighttime sounds I hear, except the creak or two each time I shift my weight. There are no springs within this mattress, but there are creaking noises none the less.

There was a motel bed in Aspen that was very bad. I think the management supplied the maids with watering cans to keep the bedsprings rusty. That is a funny thought. Ha ha. Perhaps I'll write it on a card and send it off to Bailey: *"Hi, Bailey. I am in the Always Rusty Motel, so named because the maids each morning sprinkle water on the bedsprings...."* He would peer down over his half specs and make his good large grin, and he would use the line to make some woman laugh the next time he moteled it. That is good. Laughing can't hurt.

There is barely light to see. I am tired of the blasted moon. It is still there, hovering near the horizon like a buzzard. If this is now the middle of the night, why is the moon not in the middle of the sky? There are some

questions left like that which puzzle me, like why the card I
plan to send to Bailey says, *"I am in the Always Rusty
Motel...."* I am not in the Always Rusty Motel. I am not in a
motel at all. I did not sign a registration card tonight, or
cash a traveler's check to pay my bill, or have to wonder at
the wonderful variety of types who find the call in Motel
Management.

Twice now I've heard a car far off and maybe heading
down the road to me. Perhaps it was the wind. Both times
the twinge of expectation brought a chill into the Volkswagen. The quilt no longer seems so warm. There is a faint
familiar smell that I have finally identified as grass.
Perhaps there is a stash to find when morning comes. My
consciousness could stand a bit of alteration.

No real arrangements were agreed upon.

"I'll be back with a tow truck as soon as I can,"
Benjamin said. It had taken both his hands to get me in the
side door of the camper.

He slid behind the wheel of the Porsche.

Chestnut was sitting somewhat stiffly in the passenger
seat.

"Good luck," I said.


"Good luck," the woman doctor said to me.

"Thank you."

There was a bank of phones in the clinic's foyer. I
called Sweep at the loft. He had been working a late night
gig and was still sleeping when I left. I had not told him
what I was about. We had had a false alarm before.

"We finally done dood it," I said. "I'm at the Sanger
clinic. I am definitely pregnant. We're going to be a family.
Yippee!"

Sweep said that he was going out, that he'd be home by
six. He sounded pleased to have the news. I was feeling
happy; good. There was a sense of accomplishment. I had
pressured hard to have a child—doesn't being a mother
prove that one's a woman? I have always liked the way that

pregnant women look. It's worth a seat on a city bus almost every time.

I took the 8th Street Crosstown Bus to Avenue A. There was a four-block shopping circuit that I liked to make. I missed that terribly, the shopping for treats, when we moved to the house in the country.

The butcher store was first, a good small Polish shop that featured homemade wursts and smoked pork butts. I had a yen for veal. Mack the Butcher sliced the slices from the leg for me, and pounded them. I no longer had to ask for him to do that. He called me Sarah Sunshine. I think that cost me 6 or 7 cents a pound more than the A&P. But if I had forgot my netbag carryall, I could cop a shopping bag from him for free.

I stopped at both greengrocers. At one I bought large mushrooms and shallots to saute in the rich pan drippings after quickly browning the escallops of veal in butter, and the makings for a simple salad: watercress, bibb lettuce and romaine. The other yielded up two super pears and sweet green grapes and two fat out-of-season artichokes.

The dairy store had runny Brie, and heavy cream to sauce the veal and mushrooms, and butter that got sliced from chunks the size of liquor cartons. The two old men who clerked the store would rarely miss by more than half an ounce when slicing off a pound. For cooking I would buy the butter salted; for baking I would buy it plain. The bakery next door produced a crusty loaf of round white bread for sopping up the sauce; the spice shop half a block away had Tellichery peppercorns to give the salad dressing punch and coffee beans to grind for the Melitta pot. I wanted to but couldn't find the proper words to tell a single person I was pregnant.

I took the goodies home and put two hours into cleaning up the loft before I hit the liquor store. I bought a California chablis for the cooking and an unpronounceable French wine to drink. The Asti Spumante for the fruit and cheese cleaned me out. I bummed a pack of cigarettes at the candy store to get me through.

I thought, perhaps, that Sweep might bring me flowers. Violets crossed my mind. There was a place in New York State we rented our first spring and summer and there were violets growing wild out in the woods. I had never been into the woods before. That didn't seem to bother Sweep at all. The local was afraid to visit New York City, something he had never done, but he laughed at me the day I told him that sometimes I got afraid of trees.

I should have known enough by then to buy the violets for myself. Things had been going very badly. I could not help myself. I really did expect the pregnancy to act like Librium and smooth the marriage out.

"I needed some time to think, Sarah," he said. "I'm sorry, but the timing's lousy. I don't feel right about it. Let's hold off a year."

"I'm already pregnant, Sweep. We've been working at it for ten months. Why didn't you say something before?"

"I don't know. I don't understand it. Nevertheless, the timing's lousy. Let's not have it. Please."

"What do you want me to do, say okay, that's okay with me, I'll have an abortion? I'm not going to do that. We made the decision together, and I don't think the timing's bad. If you want me to have an abortion, say so. Take the responsibility for saying so, and I'll think about it."

I screamed three times in labor; the screaming was ecstatic. I held myself to one out of five when the obstetrician made his blinding scissor cuts. I was denied the moment of the actual delivery (which I believe I earned; one scream for every hundred minutes of work should be allowed) because I did not have the strength to fight the placing of the gas mask.

The baby was a boy. He was born dead. We named him Alexander.

If Alexander had lived, I would be a Jewish mother.

The thought of childbirth leaves a bit to be desired as a sleeping pill.

I do not want to wonder whether Chestnut has disgorged her bloody baby yet.

I want my drum.

I have held the demons of New England nights at bay by making sure the voices that reside in it speak out at my command. Perhaps the demons of the west are not the same. Perhaps just concentrating on the image of my drum will lighten up the night. Perhaps I can begin with simple facts.

A simple fact: My drum is red clay.

Another simple fact: The bowl-shaped top sits on a graceful neck. The quick red fox jumps over the lazy dog. Dah didlely dah da, didlely doop.

A not so simple fact: I had thought from the sound of the drum that it was actually quite big until I took its measure. It is exactly twelve inches high, seven and three-quarters inches in diameter at the top, four and one-quarter inches in diameter at the bottom of the neck.

A goatskin head is stretched across the top. It is glued to the rim, with one-half inch of skin left lapping. My doctor left a lap of flesh when he repaired me after childbirth.

If you invert the *drum* and hold it securely by the ankles, you will see that this lapping edge looks folded up and crimped in the manner of a stingy frozen piecrust.

If you reinvert the drum you will see that holes are punched in the skin directly above this rolled edge; and I could feel my doctor take his five episiotomal scissor cuts.

The Holes above the Lapping Rolled Edge of the Goatskin Head of my DRUM are spaced at fairly even intervals of one and five-eighths inch. I believe the measure that I use is accurate. It is necessary now and then to trust. I trust the leather thong that laces through the holes in the edge of the goatskin head of my drum, over and under the support thong that girds the neck, forming a zigzag pattern not unlike slip glaze designs on some American Indian pottery, although Will said the drum had come from Ethiopia.

A second leather support thong circles the bottom of
the neck of my drum. A further thong stretches between the
upper and lower supports, making four tepee shapes, and
small flat pieces of dark brown leather, shaped like
teardrops, can be used like zipper tabs—it is good to be
precise—to bring these pairs of thongs together, or open
them up, to compensate for the changes in humidity. On
damp days, when the center of the drum is hard to find, I
use the leather tabs to tighten up the head.

I have seen a photograph or two of middle-Eastern clay
drums where the heads are laced on such as this, and
another of a jungle child incised with geometric patterns
on his forehead.

My third-grade teacher was named Miss Hudson. She
liked to show us pictures of her cats. She had three of them.
Two were Siamese. She prized their crossed eyes. The third
she called a Domestic Tabby.

"Sarah has asked why people have different color
skin," Miss Hudson said. "That is a good question. People
from Europe have white skin and are called Caucasians.
People from Africa have dark skin and are called Negroes.
People from Asia have yellow skin and are called Orientals.

"In Africa there are lions and tigers and elephants. In
Asia there are also elephants, and snakes called cobras that
stand on their bellies and puff out their necks and spit
poison.

"Civilization comes from Europe, where thousands of
years ago the Greeks and Romans made great works of art.
Has anyone seen a picture of a building called the
Colosseum?"

It is not the dark before false dawn. The moon has just
retreated momentarily behind a cloud, and I have been
adreaming. I am awake and walking city streets, crazy
angled tilted streets with garish signs and rough wood
pilings fronting rubble at strategic corners where once
large buildings stood but stand no more. I recognize a

storefront now and then, a street name. The movie theatre
is a pile of frescoed plaster chunks and mildewed purple
velvet seats behind its intact columned front which is held
in place by three large beams that chance had fall at angles
of support. The marquee flashes MO E   AVE  in amber
lights. A block away a large department store which
features female mannequins made obscene by being draped
in white bed sheets survives. One window spills high-
colored shining costume jewelry from pirates' chests onto a
man-made beach of sand and gleaming metal shells.

I break the glass and crawl inside. The feel of the sand
against the flesh of my palm is exquisite. I run my hand
quite gently on the top and smooth it out. I scoop and
dribble small unstructured mounds. I do not need to make
a castle. There are no parents watching me.

The man-made shells of burnished metal are incon-
gruously bullet shaped, the color uniform. The shells of
nature speak of larger things. There is a three-foot giant of
a clam from South Pacific waters, six graduated coral
lipped whelks, a handful each of thumbnail slipper shells
and tiny well-formed rice shells neatly placed to show
contrast in size. There are grey and gold metallic jingles
that sound like muted bells when shaken in the hand, and
ordinary ashtray scallop shells made precious with fan-
tastic growths of barnacles that look like flower gardens
made of porcelain. There are cowries that have retained the
sound of where they've been and cowries pierced and strung
and used as money by the natives of the Sudan and spindle
shells and cones, the univalve majestic nautilus of Oliver
Wendell Holmes, bivalve oysters split apart and many
random halves rejoined in sculptures known as oyster beds
to stun the eye.

There is a single specimen unknown to Conchologists.
It is purple, gold and blue, with colors bright as Christmas
tinsel, conical in shape, with a brilliant spot of red in the
center of the top. Incised along the inner lip is a series of
circles, dots and lines. All mathematics can be built from
this. The lines are spectrum colored. The background is

cloud white. I hold it to my ear. The timeless secret of the
universe is caught inside this shell. I dash it down. I would
rather play with sand. But I cut my hand against a piece of
window glass and know that I must leave.

The beauty of the shell game is insidious.

It would grab away my time.

I do not know which way to go. There is a treasure
chest quite near. I take a large brass coin to toss. It says,
"Go right."

I ignore instructions.

Why should I trust a large brass coin?

I climb a rising street that leaves the city proper
trailing out behind me. There is a cold breeze blowing. I
turn and catch the view behind me by surprise.

Someone has taken my life and chopped it up and
thrown it down before me like the pieces of a doll's town
shaken to a fury in a giant's dice box.

I don't know what I'm doing here. It makes no sense at
all, like Will coming around the night before I split with
his hands empty and his cock soft to tell me he was not
going to sleep with me any more because the only time he
saw me smiling was in bed, that he was going to marry the
lolita and would I wish him well.

"Sure. Good luck," I said.

"Thanks," he said.

"Do you still want to borrow that fifty bucks you asked
for yesterday?"

"I'm not a prostitute," he said.

I think it is a Sunday. There is no way of knowing. No
prize at the bottom of the box for being right, no hint in the
touch of palm flesh to flesh. Left breast flesh. There is sure
nothing quite like the cold awakening, nothing quite like
finding a body part that feels different from the way it did
the last time that you looked.

With my right hand tucked into my left armpit, the
thumb at a right angle toward the driver's seat of the

camper, the greatest pressure lies on the line defined along my pinkie and the bottom of my palm.

I must remember to buy medical insurance. If I buy medical insurance I will get a shiny new dark purple-brown simulated leather cardboard desk calendar in the mail each year from the insurance company. I will know when it is Sunday if I keep track of the Fridays and the Saturdays. I can buy medical insurance. I don't need to know very much for that. Mostly I need a name. Need a name to play the game.

Slowly, with the balls of my fingers, I begin the exploration for a breast lump. It is never easy to do. I was taught that it was wrong to touch myself.

Sarah Fay Cohen

Sarah F. Cohen

Sarah Cohen

Mrs. Bertram Campbell

Mrs. Sweep Campbell

Sarah Campbell

Sarah Fay Campbell

Sarah Cohen Campbell

S. F. Cohen Campbell

"Hello, my name is S. F. Cohen Campbell. I am presently residing in a Volkswagen camper for reasons that are a little complicated to try and explain. I would like to buy some medical insurance."

What am I waiting for. Isn't that easy?

My left breast sags to the left. I am lying on my back. What the devil does a lump feel like anyway? Nothing really hurts, there are just some swellings that feel sore. At what wonderful magical moment does a swelling earn the name of lump? I suspect the point is virtually the same as when a knoll becomes a hill.

And why do I forget? This ritual happens to me every month.

I am steady like a rock.

I am right on schedule.

# Chapter 3

What am I waiting for? There are things that need doing. I have never had a massage, or made a guitar sing. I do not speak Russian. I have never tasted snails, or seen a sunset in the thin air of Tibet, tuned in to tabla rhythms floating toward the verandah where I sit, feet propped against a bannister, smoking a pipeful of dark and resinous hash.

I have tossed away too many hours denting a lumpy mattress.

Did I really stand outside this vehicle and watch that perfect couple disappear into the dark last night?

Did the woman named Chestnut release her fetal waters on the Porsche's passenger seat, no room for me, before they found a hospital?

How long does it take to have a baby?

I want out of here.

I prop up on an elbow.

A home-made window finished with cavetto molding has been cut into the metal here behind the driver's seat. I have never seen the likes of it before. There is a madras curtain on a string which can be closed.

The view outside the window is not to be believed. There is not even a telephone wire in sight. There is mist in this early morning light. In the far distance, purple mountains ominous. There is no sand. It is not the desert, and I am alone. Toot-toot.

The camper has been furnished with a sense of home in mind. The plywood slab on which the mattress lies extends to form a table surface. Two bright red metal plates, enameled cups and silverware are in a yellow plastic tub. There is no sign of food.

I am facing what was once the reardoor exit of the truck, which exit has been sacrificed for room. A short brass closet rod is jammed with hanging clothes. A bamboo curtain hides the bottom of the door. A guitar case painted with a scene pastoral and labeled *Chestnut* occupies a neat space in the corner. It points to a pegboard dangling strands of beads and earrings. It hangs like a painting cattycorner from where I lie. The ceiling of the truck is painted day-glo striped. A beaded curtain separates the driver's seat from me. There is a pile of books with a copy of Adelle Davis' *Let's Eat Right to Keep Fit* on top. There is a box marked "Dirty Clothes" and a covered garbage can on the high-pile carpet of maroon. There are drawers beneath the mattress platform. I reach down and open one. Proud Papa wears boxer shorts.

I hate men who wear boxer shorts.

I hate woman who can keep their homes in order.

I am up and moving.

Big deal.

I am still in a stranger's vehicle, tilted useless in a ditch.

My presence is not subtle.

I step on and break a pair of mirrored sunglasses.

The side-door handle pulls up, not down. It takes a second to figure it out. It takes a bit longer to get outside. No wonder there was trouble with the vehicle exchange last night. The angle of the decline to the little ditch is actually quite steep.

The ground looks firm on the other side of the ditch.

I judge the distance, close my eyes and jump. Why not? It is as good a way as any, if one lands on one's feet.

There are New York plates on the Volkswagen.

It is godawful chilly for Arizona. The air is dry. I walk perhaps a hundred feet and take a leak. To my right is a small outcropping of rocks. There is yucca and some stuff that might be sage. Rivulets form in the parched soil.

There is a bit of trouble with my entrance back into my temporary home. I use the top of the open door as a hold and swing one leg across. I am straddling the ditch. I transfer the weight to the leg inside the truck, lower myself as far as my arms will let me, then let go and plop down onto the floor. I crab on back and bring my other leg inside.

Mission accomplished.

Sure hope I don't get the runs.

I close the truck door to keep out the chill.

It is time to look for food.

I rifle the glove compartment. There is an assortment of maps, half a Mounds bar, which I eat, a flashlight with dead batteries, a parking ticket from the friendly city of Chicago, a joint—toot-toot—in an otherwise empty Camel pack, which I light with a book of Ted's Diner matches, two celadon glazed pottery doo-dads which feel good in the hand. There is an unused passport for one Chestnut Godfeld. She is a nineteen-year-old Hallowe'en baby. The grass is fine. The registration certificate is in the name of Carl B. Godfeld. That doesn't figure. Proud Papa-to-be with his long hair and thin dark beard introduced himself as Benjamin. Is Benjamin his middle name? The address in New York City is in the block where Sweep lives, where the loft is, where we lived together before I moved into the house.

That figures.

Sweep is the last person I feel like thinking about.

What did he see in me, anyway, that man who taught me how to laugh?

I was a flat-chested bra and a two-piece red dress with a

pleated skirt, blue piping at the neck and buttons down the back the day we met. There were black rimmed glasses and a switch neatly covering my own long hair.

I know only the feelings that I felt: a change in the level of energy. A jump in time. A looseness. The potential for commitment to be honored. That there were to be good firsts that day.

We drove through the streets of New York in Sweep's open beat-up convertible. He offered me grass in a small briar pipe with a black stem.

He took me to the Botanical Gardens in the Bronx. Sweep takes great pleasure in watching things grow. He cut a moth cocoon from an ailing tree and burned it in the shelter of some rocks. His daring quite undid me.

I unpinned the switch myself.

"Come up and I'll play my saxophone for you," he said. I was feeling bold and reckless.

"Sure."

There was a double bed.

He played me music that I did not understand because I had not had the feelings and made us dinner that I did not taste because it was not food I hungered for. He gave me more good grass and smiled me credit for Coleman Hawkins' work, the utterly disturbing *The Gilded Hawk* album I put on the turntable. I wasted agony on that selection. I was picking blind. I did not see that I could not have chosen badly. I was selecting from Sweep's taste.

He asked me, yes, and I said yes. There is no patent on that word. We undressed ourselves. I had been made to feel guilty for having sex organs. I had to close my eyes to let him look at me.

There is no way to take the love when it is offered if the feelings are misplaced.

I knew enough; I faked an orgasm.

# Chapter Four

I am seduced into mobility. Adelle Davis' *Let's Eat Right to Keep Fit* is a scary book. I scrunch behind the wheel of the camper and check the dame out in the mirror. My tongue is cracked down the center and coated with white; there is a waviness to the shape of the edge. I am deficient in the complex B vitamins. Which deficiency do I work on first?

There is a pimple on my chin. It takes me by surprise. I have not been checking in with mirrors lately. If I let it go for two weeks at a time the changes are quite visible these days.

Ah, well.

I traded my virginity for a pimple on the back of a Korean veteran. Fair enough. It was the best one I've ever seen. It came for a semester. The vet was in love with a dark-haired girl in a white sweater. (He showed me the photograph often.) It was a tight short-sleeved sweater with ribbing. The girl's head tilted up, pulling the neck skin taut. It made a demand—to be kissed?—to be strangled? I was jealous of her chest. She had really nice ones. I wiped between my legs and examined my once-and-only hymen blood. He slumped behind the wheel, eyes averted. "I'll marry you if you're pregnant," he said finally; a sob caught but did not make it. Ahh, to have replied, "Don't worry, my boobs will grow if I am." We were parked behind a billboard. Hi, John.

I left college to work. The second was boss at the job. He was married and wore jockey shorts. The last I heard he was a V.I.P. at C.B.S. Hi, Freckles. Get in touch.

The third was a pale brown skeptic. He had a soul. We shared a phone in the office. He tied me up; I tied him up; it was an experience. Hi, Gordon. Still hitting the gin?

The first Bill taught me how to blow. I picked him up on 8th Street. A last fling. N.Y.U., I am here! And he turned me on. Oh, lordie, lordie, I was running free in the green field. *April is the force that through the widening gyre....*

He split. I found my way to Pennsylvania. Doc Spenser did a good abortion. Nice old man. I had three hundred dollars. Tuition. He charged me eighty.

The one before Bailey cooked buck-o-nine steaks in a 6th Avenue joint. He slipped me free coffee. I lent him two hundred dollars. He called once, months later, after a trip to Florida with his mother. He'd visited a whore. "God, it was something, Sarah. Got it up there really straight. You'd have appreciated it."

Enough.

I give a vicious squeeze and the pimple explodes its head against the mirror. I work at it a long time, until clean blood runs.


I find the amenities!

They have been hidden behind the bamboo curtain and in the space beneath Chestnut's guitar case. There is a battery-operated Sony tape recorder with an auxiliary cigarette-lighter plug, a large box and a small box of tapes, a set of AKC headphones, grass, Bambu papers and a small vial of miscellaneous pills and capsules in a Prince Albert tin, and a brown and tan Coleman cooler with a quotation from the *I Ching* taped to the top:

### THE CORNERS OF THE MOUTH

This hexagram is a picture of an open mouth; above and below are the firm lines of the lips, and between them the opening. Starting with the mouth, through which we take food for nourishment, the thought leads to nourishment itself.

> Perseverance brings good fortune.
> Pay heed to the providing of nourishment
> And to what a man seeks
> To fill his own mouth with.

I want some leftover medium-rare T-bone steak, a cold baked potato with sour cream and a tossed green salad with Roquefort dressing.

The cooler holds a plastic bowl of brown rice cooked without salt, two containers of yoghurt, a cucumber and a bag of carrots. There is a wet bag of sprouting mung beans and a bottle of apple juice.

I must learn to suppress the anticipations to avoid the disappointments.

I exercise control over my life.

I skip a meal.

I'm flipping into weird again.
Pecker, dickie, ding dong bell.
Wham, Stir, Thank you, Sir.
I've got the Where-did-the-Morning-Go Blues.
Sometimes I'll settle for a laugh.

I did a survey on lubricants. Vaseline was the clear favorite over Wildroot Cream Oil (wrong smell), Brylcreem (too greasy), peppermint flavored toothpaste (feels like pins and needles and is hard to wash off) and moisturizing creams and conditioners that tighten away wrinkles.

Wesson Oil was a close second.


A dealer friend of Viking's came with some grass. He really gave me the eye.

"How many men have you slept with?" he asked.

"Take a guess."

"Nineteen," he said.

I found a good look. "You hit it right on the head," I told him. "That's incredible. You're very perceptive, aren't you."

It was good for a free ounce.


I need to go over this one one more time.

Here I am, Sarah Sarah Sarah, a normal, overweight, adult Jewish woman who is sitting on the floor of a blue Volkswagen camper, stuck in an ordinary ditch in a part of southern Arizona not even inhabited by Indians, eating a carrot.

What's so unusual about that?

And what am I waiting for, anyway? Prince Charming in a snorting white repair truck? A Sir Galahad to call me Grail? Grail Cohen Campbell. Not bad. It has a ring. Like the most deadly of the poisonous Amanita mushrooms. Does it matter that other distinguishing features of those mushrooms have been named by men as the veil and vulva? Of course not.

I scream from my diaphragm and the bottom of my lungs.

Echoes are not the same the second time around.


My marriage was good for a long time. Sweep was great to take along. He had once met Mick Jagger. I never tired of hearing the story, especially when conversation in a group had stopped.

He would trot it out on cue.

"What kind of a game are you playing, anyway?"
Sweep asked me once.

"I'm not playing a game."

There is no game if there is no reality.

Sweep had once met Jagger; I experienced meeting
Sweep.

There are twinges in my stomach. I will need a diner
before dark. A bathroom serviced by a Rest Rooms
Institute, smelling of cinnamon disinfectant with a full-
sized Ex-Ternal Sanitary Belt with Pad dispenser.

My first egg-of-the-month took the chance the winter I
was fifteen. I served hard waiting time. The words had all
been tried out in the locker room and I was getting close to
last. I think that laurel went to...what was her name?

Menstruation is an enormous first. I would like to have
an enormous first be *right* for me some day. There were
cramps in my stomach and a lightness like a dizzy spell.
How much of that was actually physical? There is an eerie
echo walking empty yellow-tiled school halls when classes
are in session. Three scary gentile football-playing boys
were in the nurse's office.

"What is it, Sarah?" the nurse said.

It didn't show. "I think I have a period," I said.

"What?"

I identified the sound from one of the boys. It was a
snicker.

"I have my first period. I don't know what to do."

I was taken into the small room with the bed. "I'm
surprised at you, Sarah," the nurse said. "That is a very
private matter and should not be discussed publicly."

I had allowed myself to run the phantasies. I thought it
was possible to bleed to death. Is death a private matter?

I was given a sanitary belt and pad. I did not know
how to use them. At home I was given a slap across the face.
It is a ritual Jewish custom.

"No, we're not animals. We're civilized."

I guess I owe some dues. There is no such thing as a free roof.

I will put the vehicle in even better order.

It has been a long time. My skill at the trade of cleaning leaves a lot to be desired. It took a long time even learning to wash dishes. It helps, when washing dishes, if one thinks of taking cock.

I lower myself to the floor and check through Daddy's drawer: there is nothing there that interests me, but the other drawer is quite a different matter. There are four folded pieces of paper, two empty Hershey-with-Almonds bar wrappers, which I check out for crumbs, a fringed leather vest and, in a canvas laundry bag, a mess of black slinkies: three bras, one with cut-out nipple holes, three pairs of long black stockings, one with runs, a garter belt with six garters, a narrow corset with bone stays, a couple of lace-edged half slips. Indeed. Chestnut must have really loved it when her body started going to waist.

I unfold the pieces of paper. Three are jottings written in Chauncery Cursive calligraphy with brown ink: *"There was an excitement about her that intrigued him, and he tingled with desire over his omelet and coffee"; "All speculation rewards the self"; "It is worth taking risks for the feeling of intimacy."*

The fourth is a letter:

*Dear Benjamin:*

*There is a block that arises inside me when I sit down to write a letter to someone I love. It comes in the form of a strong negative rejection of that person and the ideas that were in mind when the idea of composing a letter arose. I feel it as strongly as if someone were to touch me then. It comes automatically and without my will from years of reaction to possible love/hate relationships that were offered and proved, by bitter experience, to have been so hurtful as to be intolerable.*

*Nevertheless, I love you as much as possible. I*

> *am afraid of it because it is carrying me into*
> *uncharted waters where there are unknown*
> *dangers. Unknown dangers are the most*
> *frightening.*
>
>                                        *Love,*
>                                        *Chestnut*

It is snowing hard. I have put on the tree lights—there were
no Christmas trees in my house growing up. The house is
almost clean and toasty warm. There is a fire going in the
chunk stove. The thermostat for the oil burner is up to 68°.

There is a six-pound standing rib roast in the oven,
two loaves of oatmeal-raisin bread well cooled on racks. I
had baked a dark fruit cake a month before. There is
eggnog waiting for the beaten egg whites to be folded in.
Sweep is due with Bailey and a date and a couple of
musician friends at 5:00. He calls at 7:00, still in New York,
drunk at the club.

I am snowed in alone for three full nights, two days.
Will found a bulldozer; he got the driveway reamed.

I have always had a thing for gentile men. I have not
had a single Jewish lover since my teens. I think that is
because we had no Christmas trees in my house growing
up. My mother passed along the clannish Jewish prohibi-
tions very well; it took a gentile cock to get me.

I held off sleeping with Will for more than another
month. There is the power of taboos within a wedding
ring. I had, after all, bought the ring myself.

There was no excuse, was there?

Was it worth it, you fucking hole between my legs?

I replace the things that I have taken from the drawer
beneath the mattress platform and with a flourish push it
home.

It will not close.

I never did learn how to close drawers. It drove Sweep
crazy. When we moved into the house I made a stab at it.

"Look, I do the best I can." I told him. "I don't complain when you spend two hours practicing long tones. I've learned to cook like a trooper, I put the toilet paper in the holder the right way and I recap the toothpaste. Drawers are very hard. I'm restructuring as fast as I can."

"You're a grown woman, Sarah."

How come he didn't remember that on my birthdays, when I needed it?

I pull the drawer out and slam again.

I knew that Will would bring me off. He had that power aura of self-centeredness about him. A come-and-get-me cockiness that says "I set the rules." I needed that. An outside place to do the battle with my demons. It is a fast way through for me.

He did it with three fingers shoved high up and hard inside my cunt. There was no tenderness at all. He laced me open with his tongue at first, hands crossed across my stomach, arms holding tight against my bent up thighs, preventing a retreat. My phantasies protected me like pop-up arcade figurines. I sounded so that outside ears would hear that I was still alive.

"That's a first," he told me.

"How do you know?"

"I know," he said.

I pull the drawer out one more time and slam. It does not relent. I work it free of its housing and get on my knees. The blood rushes to my head and my back protests. I am hauling around a lot of weight.

Blocking the drawer is a cardboard box, dark grey, about the size of a shoebox and the shape of a trunk. It contains a pair of handcuffs in a red velvet jewelry box, a bank-type Manila envelope with the ashes of what must have been a large number of letters, and a small leather-bound manuscript book, the title page of which reads *The Power Struggle*. The handwriting is Chauncery Cursive Calligraphy. I toss the book on the mattress.

I replace the drawer in the housing and push it home.
I have learned how to close a drawer.
I make a decision for the future.
Floor work is out.

# *Chapter Five*

## THE POWER STRUGGLE

My lover kneels before me.
Fully clothed.
Forty-one, perhaps.
I shall make him six feet tall.
"You are a witch," he says.
He strokes a hand across one velvet-covered thigh.
He teases his tongue along my inner arm.
The skin of my thigh is really quite soft.
He tosses his head, which tousles his hair. I could grab his hair in handfuls hard and bring his eager tongue where I would have it, moving now...

moving now...

moving now...

Take it easy, Chestnut.
There is a lot of time.
I send him off for brandy.

My lover brings me brandy. He kneels before me, fully clothed. Forty-one. Dark tousled hair.
"You are a witch," he says.
I laugh and toss my head.

He rises, holds me in the pose, firm hand upon my
neck.

I run my palms along my velvet-covered thighs.

"Wait," he says.

I wait.

My lover kneels before me, fully clothed. He calls me
witch, and dares to touch my thigh.

I will not move for him.

My long soft velvet skirt, autumn midnight navy
blue, falls open to the knee.

Lord, listen to Duane Allman play that magic steel
guitar!

I place two fingers on my clit and let the music take
me.

My lover stills my hand.

He laughs.

"You are a hot bitch cunt," he says.

He brings me supple leather boots.

They come to the tops of my thighs.

I am an animal.

I put one leather-covered foot upon my lover's knee.

"It would alter things to see you crawl."

My silken shirt unbuttons to the waist.

My lover teases me.

He touches one thumb to the edge of one breast.

"You are very strong and beautiful," he says. "I could
punish you for that."

I bring my lover brandy and stand between his
thighs.

My velvet skirt unbuttons to the waist.

My lover humors me.

He lets me see his thick hard cock.

My lover brings me perfume for my breasts and garters for my boots.

"I am afraid of the perfume."

"Learn to use it. It is a tool."

I wear puce silk and purple velvet, black leather boots and perfume at my wrists.

I bring my lover oranges and Tokay grapes on silver German pewter.

I have made a potion.

No bitter taste.

Thyme from the garden. Sage.

"It is not true," I tell him. "The edges of my cunt are smooth."

My lover lays his hand across my gentle stomach curve. He dares to look me in the eye.

"I will only hurt you with my penis."

I dance before my lover in the heat of the late afternoon sun.

I head to the edge of the bright green field. There is dark forest on the other side.

He follows slowly. A leather collar and a leash are in his hand.

"You have too much energy," he says. "I will restrain you."

"Come dance with me."

"I can not. I am afraid the dance will kill you."

I make food for my lover.

I spice with mace and nutmeg.

He should never trust me so.

I do not know my lover's name.

Carl will do.

I tease my lover, Carl. Carl.

He kneels before me, fully clothed.
He will rub his tongue soft circles on my clitoris!
I run a hand between my legs and rub the smell across my upper lip.
I lick the moisture with my tongue.

Carl rubs his tongue soft circles on my clitoris.
It is too intense.
It feels like pain.
I move away from him. Control. Control.
His fingers work the buckle of his belt.
"You must learn to tolerate the pleasure."
I am afraid.

I have new clothes today. Slew a large dumb beast. Fashioned the skin.

My lover looks at what I've done.
"You make me want you when you do good work," my lover says.
I am excited by the news.
My nipples stand erect.

My lover Carl removes my skin tight shirt. He turns me slowly round; one hand secures my wrists.
Carl pulls aside his tunic top: Great hanging alabaster tulip woman breasts.
"Shit, piss, rag, twat, they say my next-door neighbor's brother sucks his thumb!"
I am gagged with bitter canvas by my lover, forty-one.

I am caught.
There is no room to run.
I fight.
I do the best I can....

My lover joins my ankles to my wrists as if with cold link chain.

I arch like a bow.

I am suspended by my feet.
The blood rushes to my head.

I am stretched upon the rack.
My muscles are very lazy.

I am fastened to a cross.
I am aware.

My lover holds my wrists to my crossed thighs.
I am open like a Lotus.

"It is as if you have learned everything I know," my
lover says.
I feel whipped upon the back with the lash of the
compliment and scream.
All sound flows from throat to diaphragm.
I have found my voice.
I am invincible.
I writhe on the stake for howling like a witch.

Carl holds and rides the wave with me. Magenta
purple cock. Rain forests on the flank. I pull away. I am
afraid of the dying.
"You are strong enough to take it. I am strong
enough to have you."
Great echoing cathedral screams.
Cold breath.
"Your cervix cups my penis like a chalice."
My lover lies upon my breasts. My hands are on his
back.
It feels like my flesh.


Benjamin approaches.
And it is high goddamned time. I have spent myself. I
am hungry. I am thirsty. I have been lying listless on this

mattress way too long. I am up a tree, screwed, fucked, nailed, pronged, bored by an auger to tears with it all. How does one learn to tolerate the pleasures if it takes so long to recognize pain grey?

But I can not think about it any more just now. It is nearly dark and I know my ordeal is coming to an end. There is no way for the Porsche to take me by surprise—not here, not in this open desert space where sound carries so that surely Benjamin will hear the beating of my heart.

I have been struck with the premonition that Chestnut has died giving birth to a baby boy who lives. That instructions have been given to name the baby Alexander. That I am caught in a cosmic coincidence from which I shall never be free. Have I dared ignore too many of the *déjà vus*? Is that my sin?

There is a polite knock on the side door of the Volkswagen.

"It's open," I say, and rearrange myself as Benjamin returns.

He climbs in the door and comes to occupy the space I have vacated by sitting up. He hands me the keys to the Porsche. It is hard to assign change to his face; the colors in the air are changing rapidly; we have reached the point where twilight becomes dusk. He muddles his hand through the hair above his right ear.

"Chestnut's dead, isn't she," I say.

"Yes. She died at six o'clock this morning." No surprise. No "How do you know?" No tears. No further information.

I can not phrase a question that is adequate. I do not know exactly what it is I want to know. Can I say, Is Alexander all right? Do I dare risk this? The impli—

"The baby's a girl. She's fine. Six pounds, four ounces. All her fingers and toes." He leans over and begins to play with the beaded curtain behind the driver's seat. "I'm sorry it took me so long to get back."

"That's all right."

"I don't know what's happening. 'You have a daughter

to think of, Mr. Godfeld,' " Benjamin says, obviously mimicking someone at the hospital. "I've been driving around for hours. I thought about just taking off with your Porsche. That's a really nice car."

"I understand."

"You do? That's nice."

And suddenly there are beads, beads everywhere, and Benjamin is keening a high-pitched wordless song that reminds me of the moon, and he has flung open the camper door to let in the dark night air, and he has pulled a load of dresses from the rack and has tossed them out upon the ground. The pegboard and the jewelry hanging on it follow suit. I stop him when he reaches for the guitar.

"Don't," I say. "Don't do that."

"Why? Do you want it?"

"Sure!"

"Okay. Get it out of here. I don't ever want to see it again. And this too, and these." He hands me the guitar, a small manuscript book marked *Love Songs—Chestnut Godfeld*, and the small box of tapes.

"She spent hours every day playing her guitar. I couldn't bear to have it around. She'd fool around with the tuning pegs until she said the strings 'sounded right' and then she'd start attacking them with a pick until she got a rhythm going, and then she'd start singing her songs. She sang all the time. Sometimes she'd sing all the words of the Love Songs every day for weeks, and the melodies were different every time."

"I understand."

"You understand? How could you possibly understand? How could you possibly understand?"

"Look, Benjamin, I'm sorry Chestnut's dead, but I don't know you at all and I'm hungry and I'm thirsty and I'm tired and I'd like to get into town and find a motel. You are going to have to tell me if there is anything I can do to help you, because I have got to get out of here."

"Okay. Go ahead. I'm not stopping you."

"Yes, you are. I can't just leave you."

"Why not? We just left you here last night."

"That was different."

He emits a short, bitter laugh. "That's the kind of line that would have made Chestnut start writing a song," he says. "She'd make up funny little songs all the time."

"I have a friend who earns a living writing songs," I venture. "His name's Bailey Gorsham."

"She never wanted to make money from her songs," Benjamin says. "She did it because she had to. She couldn't read or write music. She said maybe she'd learn after the baby so she could....The baby's a girl, you know. Chestnut said if it was a girl...." He pulls a battery-operated light from some secret place I didn't find and turns it on. "I've got to pick up her things," he says. "A girl will want her mother's jewelry. Please get the guitar out of here."

"Do you want me to wait for you?" I say.

"I don't know," he says. "I don't know what to do. How can I possibly know what to do? I'm only twenty-one years old."

"That's very young to be a widower," I say.

I regret the word the minute that I speak it, but it sets us both in action. Benjamin helps me out the door, puts the guitar on the hood of the Porsche, and begins to retrieve and reassemble Chestnut's wardrobe. I hold the light for him. We work in silence until the job is done.

"I think I'd like to stay here tonight," he says at last.

"Are you sure that's a good idea?"

"I don't know," he says. "But that's what I want to do. Do you think you could arrange for a garage to send a tow truck in the morning?"

"All right."

"I'll see you to the Porsche," he says, and takes my arm, leaving me no choice. Some part of me feels great reluctance at this parting. I think I have begun to bleed.

We hesitate beside the Porsche.

"I wouldn't mind at all if you change your mind about the guitar," I say.

"No, I'd like you to have it," he says. "What's your last name, Sarah?"

"Campbell."

"That's right," he says. "You told me that last night."

"Okay," I say. "You'll be okay. I'll send someone first thing in the morning. There's a little bit of rice left in the cooler. I didn't eat it all."

He is holding the guitar. I am inexplicably moved to tears.

"I need a few minutes more," he says. "I need to play it just one time. Chestnut used to try and get me to play it, but I wouldn't." He sits on the ground in front of the Porsche and takes the guitar from the case. He removes a piece of grey plastic that is threaded in the strings.

"She just got this pick last week," he says. "She said it sounded like fuzzy monsters. Fuzzy monsters."

He strikes the pick across the guitar, hitting all six strings in unison, again and again, setting up a simple rhythm.

"And then she'd go like this," he says, putting a single left hand finger on and then off a string. On and then off in a different place. It makes me want my drum.

"And like this"—he uses a second finger—"and this." He has put his whole index finger against the strings, and is moving his hand up and down, seemingly at random. The sound is rich and full and very interesting.

He breaks off abruptly.

"That really hurts," he says, flexing his hand.

"It sounded very nice, Benjamin."

"Please go. Please take the guitar and go."

## LOVE SONGS—CHESTNUT GODFELD

Lost in the heaven
Cryin' for the wine

Castles in the fire
Danger all the time

Drink the bitter potion
Love ain't never come to stay

Take it while you got it
Been here all day


6 a.m.
Music in my head
Got to get it up and out
Or can't get out of bed

9 a.m.
Sunlight sits like lead
Brandy bottle stares at me
Cobwebs in my head

No toadstools in the garden
Cat went and died
Two o'clock in the afternoon
Lonely inside

Nine o'clock in the evening
Darkness comforts me
Fantasy lover comes at ten
He finds what is left of me


Phantom voices in a whirlpool wind
Flushed a grouse at noon.
Aluminum sun in a pearl-grey sky
Say lover coming soon.

Mildew blots my dreaming
Heart pains in my head
Lover didn't come today
Wish he were dead.

Time weighs me down like chain mail
Wrinkles round my eyes
Put up my purple velvet gown
Make poison for the flies.

A wind is blowing through me
Night forests in my black hair
Sandstone canyons in my thick slow blood
Time to take another trip out there.

Where they're talking bad about me:

Say I shattered ice on the lake at three
That I'm killing off all the grain
That I caused the fever in nine fine sons
And poisoned six daughters' brains.

Yellow line in the center of the road
Pulling on me
Pressures wrinkles into my skin;
Pressures downward on my knee.

Speed dims the need for headlights.
Trees roll backwards into Friday's noon.

Found a golden scapegoat.
Full moon.


There's a large red oak near the garden
White birches stand by its side
Lover said he might come today
Does that mean I should stay inside?

Wind whispers hot to the larches
Hunger pains on my skin
Lover said he might come today
I'm not going to think about him.

I don't wait me around for no man
No man's going to keep me inside
There are things I've got to do
With my sunny day mood
I'm not going to stay in and hide.

# PART III

# Chapter One

I shop for a snack and find a motel. It is called The Rustic Arms. I register as Annie Bodwyn Carr. I park the Porsche in front of Door 19. Thursday the 23rd of March. How did it get to be Thursday the 23rd of March?

I have been blessed with a less than perfect room. Three walls are papered yellow with red roses and the fourth is red with yellow roses. The back window faces a super highway: two gasoline stations with bright yellow signs, a McDonalds and a large brick building with no windows in the facing wall. There is a sign framed in the middle lower pane. It reads: *Speed Limit 40*. What a nice thing to say. I watch the passage of a bright orange Dodge pin-striped in black; it glints in the late afternoon sun. In the next room, a couple of guys are making it.

It is an anniversary. I am seven months on the road. Everything changes; everything stays the same. I have learned a thing or two. I remove the chenille bedspread to protect my nappy pants. It is easier than the laundromat. There is a color tv. I red in John Wayne's face. I settle down to stare and eat. I make a mistake. I am lazy and do not get up to turn off the news. Vita herring in wine sauce with onions, a box of Mallomars and the war in Vietnam don't mix.

It is hard to get drunk with an upset stomach. I pick a tape at random from the box that Benjamin gave me and put it on my brand-new portable machine. Chestnut plays her guitar, just for me, and sings. I listen for a long time. I watch the level of the Scotch recede within the bottle. It is wondrous to behold, an animation sequence on the making of a desert. I mull about the irony of Chestnut dying giving birth to a baby girl who lives.

Real rewards for real work.

There is a center to hold on to.

I am sick in the swirling blue waters of the Sanitized peach pink bathroom bowl.

I must remember to honor my mother and father for giving me the gift of life.

I gas up the Porsche and get a western map to reassure myself.

I am not going in circles.

I have returned to Colorado from the south. I came from New Mexico, which I entered from the west. That is, of course, more or less of a right angle, if I do not return to Utah, which is how I got to Arizona in the first place.

I register in the Bide-A-Wile Motel as Wilma Valentine. It is five in the afternoon. The motel's walls are plastered with travel posters: *See Sunny Spain; Gorgeous Greece; Come to Japan—Land of the Rising Sun; The Hidden Empire: Ethiopia; There is Mystery in Yugoslavia.* Yugoslavia? Is there a local red cell in this burg?

I reconnoiter for food; there is a selection of sorts. I have a BLT and home fries in a Quonset-hut diner and take out for the evening from a take-out Taco joint. Everything needs salt. The frozen custard stand is boarded closed. The liquor store is closed. The movie theatre offers a double feature: *Son of Flubber* and *Million Dollar Duck.*

I stop for a mild-looking hitchhiker. He has a well-stuffed knapsack. It is a tight fit. Chestnut's guitar has served to complicate the space inside the Porsche.

We exchange information.

The hitchhiker tells me he is visiting with friends about one hundred fifty miles due east before returning home to Omaha.

I tell him I am stopping off at points of interest before returning home to plant a garden for the summer. That is a bald-faced lie, although the thought has obviously occurred to me.

The hitchhiker offers a recent journey to the Sahara to cover the inoculation of a camel herd for hoof and mouth disease, an illness and an odyssey in search of penicillin.

I offer a tidbit about penicillin encouraging the growth of vaginal yeasts.

He offers a gem about the active principle of *Amanita muscaria*, which is the preferred, because only, hallucinogen of the Siberian indians.

I turn the hitchhiker on.

I play him one of Chestnut's tapes.

I let the hitchhiker out.

I am giddy with needs.

I register in the Wagon Wheel Motel as Buena Glissanda. A knob is missing from the nighttable drawer. I point out the cigarette burn in the carpet to the clerk. I take a shower and wash my hair.

The color is wrong in the color tv and I settle for green in the faces. I feed three quarters into the bed relaxacisor, which works just fine, and pour rum, dark, over ice cubes. I have brought a ham and onion grinder with tomatoes and cheese, a bag of taco chips and two packages of Twinkies. Claudette Colbert and Clark Gable square off. They both lose.

The grinder roll is stale. Why bother eating something that does not taste good?

I fall into a restless sleep. I dream about forsythia on the side of a steep frozen hill, full yellow on a February afternoon. The largest clump is in a bower under tough survivor elms. There is a bed of huge tiger lilies, double blossomed, the golden needles subtle to my starving tongue. A cat appears and claims he owns the flowers.

I have passed the halfway mark to thirty-four. That would be just doozy if I were a hunk of Penn Central stock. I drive north on a road blasted from the side of a rocky mountain. I have been to the desert and there is no sand. I smoke a joint and put a Chestnut tape in the machine. I approach a black double squiggle with a wide sweeping archback to the right. I down shift to take it. It is as good as promised. An eight and a half on a ten scale. I am descending from the high peaks. I must learn to Sunday drive the Porsche.

I have missed the shaggy mane mushrooms by many months this year. Sweep told me once he saw a bloom of shaggy manes destroy a three-mile stretch of road by pushing up and through macadam before their self-digesting life cycle process turned them into ink. I would like to see a sight like that some day. The late afternoon sun is playing leapfrog with purple and shadows. I toot it a salute with the Porsche horn. Who knows, it may need it.

It is late, and I cannot take it. My hands move on the wheel and I have a hunger. I have driven many miles today. The bed is a motel familiar. My flesh weighs upon me like a beef carcass on a butcher's hook. In the next room a couple is making it, the bedsprings howling like dogs with a fox at bay. I crack open the new bottle.

"Here's to you, fuckers."

Not bad, for cheap brandy.

I have had a lover or two in my time.

Some fun and games.

Will asked, "What is a whore?"

I said, "I am a whore."

It is an act of courage to accept the labels.

Did I really think he was the man with whom it would be possible to play out my games?

Toot-toot! Here is a Chestnut tape I haven't played!

Will I weigh 250 pounds in August on my birthday? I

doubt it very much. The constant of my life has been to fall
short of my goals. I will simply say I'm feeling guilty, if
anyone bothers to ask. It is less costly than describing cold
white lime deposits forming wet on grey stone tunnel
walls. It does not matter, does it?

There is a mirror on the open bathroom door. I
undress on the bed and contemplate my naked profile, head
turned. I am like the near-inflated wrinkles at the seams of
a young child's blow-up plastic punching clown.

They are still at it, my next-door neighbors, the
bedsprings loud and rhythmic, like the center beat of heavy
rock.

I am suddenly excited. I masturbate. I calculate the
orgasms. Intercourse, 47; masturbation, 4,312, give or take a
few.


The hitchhiker holds a sign. It says, "N.J. TPK. Split
gas and tolls." He is about six feet tall, long haired,
moderately clean; it is the stance that gets me, a certain
Will-like surly looseness. I think about an episode from
childhood as I pass him by.

There is no turning back.

I have conceived of a union without New Jersey.


It is nearly noon. That is as good a time as any. It has
been a while since I have played my drum. There is a
promising dirt turnoff just ahead and to my right. A well-
weathered wooden gate with a chain and rusty padlock
blocks a narrow road. I extricate my drum and sit upon a
rock to play.

I do not understand why it should be; sometimes I need
to play so much the need prevents the center voice from
speaking back to me. That used to happen to me sometimes
when I was in bed with Sweep. The touch of the hand that I
needed so much would dry my juices up.

A car stops. It is a white four-door sedan. South Dakota
plates. Two long-haired bearded wild-eyed males in gypsy
garb and paisley headbands watch me through the wind-

shield. I can not deal with it. I close my eyes and find the center of my drum. Boom a chuck a boom a chuck a car door opens boom a chuck a bout with rhythm every day helps keep the boogie men away a boom a chuck another hand drum joins me in the play and then a mouth harp comes in loud and clear—

It cracks!

The goatskin head of my red clay drum has cracked!

The strangers leave me with condolences upon my loss.

The chill of April in the Colorado noonday sun reminds me of New England mornings at the end of August when the days are ripening toward autumn.

The waitress has bleached white hair and a three-strand choker around her neck. She wears a plastic nametag above her left breast: Pearl. I ask for a menu and a glass of water. Pearl brings the menu. The water glass has lipstick on the rim.

There is a bowling foursome dressed in pastel-colored overalls sitting at the counter. Names are embroidered on the backs: Ray, Mitzi, Adelia-Sue, Joan. Two shrill, two nasal voices, getting it up for the game. Pearl stands in the aisle before the kitchen door and offers hard twangy support. My order is in the salesbook in her left hand.

"Hi! What a nice coincidence," I say. The hitchhiker's sign says "Omaha."

"Hi," the hitchhiker says. "Well, I have a friend who swears there are only fifty people in the world."

"You know, I was thinking about your *Amanita muscaria* story, about the active hallucinogenic principle being passed along in urine."

"Right," the hitchhiker says.

"I got to seeing him."

"Who?"

"The active principal. He was sitting on a wooden stool in a glass pickle barrel, immersed to his neck, naked of course, with a high fur hat on his head, drinking a glass of vodka."

I turn the hitchhiker on.

I play him another one of Chestnut's tapes.

I let the hitchhiker out.

I am giddy with needs.


It is too awkward on the bed, that's what's wrong!

I pull the straight-backed chair away from the desk and move myself around until I finally get comfortable. Chestnut's guitar is fighting with my breasts.

I give a whack at the strings with the pick, like Benjamin did. It sounds okay. I do it again. I like it even better. I get my right hand moving evenly, hitting all six strings in unison each beat. It is not unlike the way I first attacked my drum. The sound is full and loud. I get a rhythm pattern going with a single left hand finger, then let my hand slide up the neck. It sounds like a sound a guitar player would make. I get adventurous and try a second finger, and a third...the guitar is full of music! It surrounds my space and comforts me, like drum beats building rust adobe structures in the setting sun.

I could beat the labyrinth today.

I could make the clouds give rain.

I could have a....

The phone on the nighttable between the double beds is ringing. It makes me want to laugh. Are my next-door neighbors really calling to complain? They have been grunting their pleasure for hours, like pigs.

"Hello?"

"This is the manager speaking. Is this room Seven B?"

"You're at the switchboard, you tell me." I am in pain. The muscles of my left hand ache.

"Is this Miss Contra—How do you pronounce your name?"

"Contrastori. Magdalena Contrastori." The image of the aging grande dame has appeal. My fingertips are sore. When I press them with my thumb they hurt.

"I'm sorry, Miss Contrastori, but we've had a complaint about noise from your room."

"What kind of noise?"

"Guitar noise."

"Guitar noise? Guitar's don't make noise, they make music." My fingers are going to hurt when I put them back on the strings of Chestnut's guitar. It was like that with the palms of my hands when I first began to play the drum.

"I'm sorry, but I will have to ask you to stop playing or to check out. It is the policy of this motel to guarantee our guests a good night's sleep."

"They're fucking in there, you know."

"What?"

"The people next door. It's a couple of guys and a girl. Three of them. She's been moaning a lot. I think maybe they've kidnapped her."

"What!"

"Over and out."


I am sprinting when I want to rest. The road is a challenge; there are many signs of casualties. I take advantage of a passing lane and push it up to seventy. I am desperately hungry. I want the sound of a friendly human voice. I will settle for a container of coffee and a half a dozen Dunkin' Donuts.

I eat a can of Spam.


I cross the George Washington Bridge. I have been gone a good long time. They have enacted a new system that I did not know about. The cars now pay a double toll in one direction only. I would like to watch the morning rush up high some time. It must look like metal smoke being drawn into the lungs of New York City.

I ease the Porsche to the right and take the exit for the Henry Hudson Parkway north. Can I really manage to survive the reacquaintances? Can I survive without a place where I can play?

I detour beneath the bridge, debating. It is a nice trick,

the circle drive beneath the bridge. Sweep taught it to me. I like it best on summer nights when floodlights high up in the girders catch patches of thick moist grey air and haze glows canyon pink around the street lights. There is a place to stop almost beneath the bridge. Even very late at night one car and then another will cruise past from right to left, which gives a certain measure to the speed and size of things. Once chance allowed me nearly twenty minutes here before another car came around the circle curve.

The daytime traffic goes too fast to let me feel the magic of the bridge or marvel at suspension thoughts. I catch a space behind an old blue coupe and swing out to the left and north and east again.


I am caught. My appetites are not to be denied. I am in heaven, an all-night luncheonette in the middle of a variety grocery store. There is a bakery counter wafting the smell of sugared donuts, two tall whores and their pimp, two prospective customers overlapping orange counter stools, a wall of magazines and newspapers. I buy a *New York Times.*

I squeeze into a booth in a corner, my back to a wall. Less than a week and I've been thrown out of two motels for playing the guitar. I must be doing something right.

The table top is grey formica with a geometric pattern that is thermos-bottle red. I have only seen that pattern pink before. I never did find time to ask what Benjamin had named her daughter.

The whores have gotten grilled cheese sandwiches and Cokes. I order and tackle the *Times.* More women are traveling alone, some hard-nosed woman reporter reports. I decide to pay some dues. I will skip the sugar if the waitress ever brings the coffee.

Bathrooms marked with black silhouette heads on bright orange signs are on the wall to my left, separated by a large efficient-looking penny scale. There is a bank of checkout lines and a delicatessen department sporting two beautiful roasted beeves and a pineapple-topped glazed ham.

I am having trouble establishing communication. My veal arrives. It is nicely breaded but without a trace of cheese. The salad is French instead of Roquefort dressed. The spaghetti is a trifle overdone. My piece of Boston cream pie remains in the case behind the counter. No coffee.

One of the whores, steady on high heels, heads for the ladies' room and enters, ignoring the scale. The pimp has gone to talk to the two men at the counter. I read the bridge column. The finesse doesn't work. Is it trying to tell me something? The whore reappears. I have lost my appetite. I need to know how heavy I am.

I check my change purse for a penny. I check the bottom of my bag and turn up $2.35. There are two dimes and a penny in my raincoat pocket, along with some used Kleenex, two empty gum wrappers, a roll of Butter Rum Life Savers and a roach stuffed in the back of a matchbook.

I decide on a quick assault: walk directly up, step on the scale, insert coin, glance at the news, walk back to the checkout line, pay the bill and zoom away in the Porsche.

I gesture for my check. I tear the crossword puzzle from the book review page and leave the rest of the paper behind. I get off on games.

I will allow five pounds for my clothes and put my bag on the floor.

I hit the bathroom first. It is a mess and smells bad. Don't they ever clean the place? I lean against the sink and run through it again. Shit. I could have paid the bill and then walked back to the bathroom. Too bad.

The door opens inward. I pretend to be drying my hands. It is a woman in her thirties with a pleasant face wearing a pink and grey plaid dacron and polyester pants suit. She enters the stall and begins an amazing piss.

The fluorescent lights in the luncheonette have gone and gotten pea green halos. Machinery hums. I step on the scale and insert the penny in the slot. There is a tinny sound. The veil does not lift. I have been rejected for not reading the sign. We are in a galloping inflation. I fumble in my bag to find a nickle.

"Hey, would you look at that."

It is the whore with the high heels.

She is standing in the aisle with one of the johns and she is dumping it off on me.

I am burning myself out. It is a case of overkill, two hundred twenty-seven pounds. I need to talk to someone my own size about the common difficulties: on the enterings and leavings and the shortness of breath.

I am shopping for some food.

I take it aisle by aisle.

There are a lot of groovy specials: baby smoked oysters, Nabisco chocolate grahams, large ripe bright green avocados, a ten-roll package of toilet paper priced at 89¢.

I turn into the pickle aisle; half way down, at a cross aisle, a grocery boy is setting up a display of cans. A cart is stopped nearby.

I attack; I misjudge the size of the opening. I am faced with chaos, the sound of denting cans.

# Chapter Two

"Hi, Sam. I need some help. The mud's so bad I can't get into my house."

"Christ, Sarah!"

"Yeah, I know. Eighty pounds." I am grinning like an idiot. I can not help it. I am out in plain sight with Chestnut's guitar case clutched against my raincoat. "It's good to see you."

"Christ, Sarah."

"Don't you ever say anything but 'Christ, Sarah?' "

"Sorry, forgot my manners. Here. Let me take the guitar. I didn't know you had a guitar."

"You've rearranged the shop. It looks great. I got the guitar down in southern Arizona. It belonged to a woman named Chestnut. It's a long story. Look, I've got to get into my house. I'm going to bust! The whole thing's too weird. The head of my drum cracked, so I picked up Chestnut's guitar instead and the damned thing started playing for me. I've put a lot of miles on the Porsche to get here."

"Christ, Sarah, you're going way too fast. Settle down. I'll take your coat. How about some coffee?"

"No, thanks. This is ridiculous, isn't it. I come barging in out of nowhere. Eight months. Nine months. I

don't know if I can do it. I suddenly feel really nervous.
Sandra. What's Sandra going to say? Bye!''

"Nothing doing, lady. No backing out," Sam says.
"It's eight-thirty on a Sunday morning and you've got me
up and moving around. I know what it's like to be excited
about a guitar. I make the damned things.''

"That's why I came here, Sam.''

"Right. So take off your coat and get comfortable and
feel free to play. I'll go make coffee and then we'll worry
about the mud.'' He stops at the kitchen door.

"Sarah?''

"Yes?''

"I'm glad to see you.''

I subside. I get Chestnut's guitar out of its case and
stroke the pick across the strings. The sound is different
from the last time that I played. I do not like what I am
hearing. The thickest string is definitely flat. I fool around
with the tuning peg and hit the strings again.

"That's pretty wild,'' Sam says.

"What do you mean? The coffee's good. Thanks.''

"You've got the guitar in an unusual open tuning. It's
very different from the standard way guitars are tuned.''

"That's the way it came to me.''

"Oh,'' he says.

"How is everyone?'' I ask. "Sandra? Young Viking?''

"Everyone's fine. The Viking's around. He's working
for some lumber guys. Sandra and Hank are living
together.''

"You're kidding!''

"Nope.''

"What about the Broadmans?''

"They're in Boston until November. Joan comes to
visit me occasionally. Ernest is teaching a pottery work-
shop. They've rented their house to a guy named David
Spofford. You'll see him around. He's finishing up a novel
and he walks a lot. He's a classically trained flautist, but
he's very loose. We've done some nice playing. Will and
Ruth are married. They're living in New York.''

"I didn't ask about Will."

"Ye gads, Sarah. Sure you did."

I hit the strings with the pick. The fattest one has definitely improved. I fool around with the other strings, each one in turn, until the sound I know returns. It seems to make Sam nervous. He gets up and begins to putter at his workbench. He is cutting fretting wire for the neck of a new guitar.

It takes me longer than it ever has before to get my timing even, picking all six strings in unison each beat. I get a rhythm pattern going with the half-a-dozen notes and two two-finger left hand chords that I have found. A certain kind of repetition. It is all a matter of lines and structure—

"Oh, what a nice place to be in!" Sam says. He has been listening after all! He picks up his guitar. He joins me in the play. He finds a melody I had not heard. The music blends and pulses, pushes me to try new things again, again, moving, moving now....

"I've got to stop. This is scaring me and I've got new blisters," I say.

"I'm jealous," Sam says.

"I know what you mean. I'm excited. One day I don't play the guitar and the next day I play the guitar."

"You don't play the guitar, Sarah."

"Sure, I do. You just heard me."

"You don't know any chords—"

"I know two chords."

"—and that tuning is outrageous. No one is going to be able to play with you—"

"You just played with me."

"—it's too complicated."

"It's very simple. All you have to do is find and hold a rhythm."

Sometimes the things that one must do affront the basic nature of the beast. I will definitely leave the opening of my refrigerator door for last. There is a single place to sit down in the livingroom. The straight-backed chair in which I used to play my drum. A massive clean-up is in order. I suppose that I should thank the snow and mud for having kept my house from being burglarized. Bailey! His number is in my mental directory. Why not? He picks up on the second ring. Toot-toot.

"Hi, Bailey."

"Sarah! You crossed my mind this morning! Where are you?"

"I'm home. I just found myself thinking the word 'burglarize' and it reminded me of you. You gave me a wonderful dressing down once for using one of those 'ize' words. Verbalize. I checked it out in the *Random House Dictionary* later, by the way. They treated it like a real word."

"As if it were a real word. And everyone knows you can't trust the *Random House Dictionary*. The word 'musician' is misspelled on page thirty-four. How are you?"

"Fat and manic. Walking into the house was a shock. I hadn't anticipated the scene. The mice have had a heyday and the damn place smells and everywhere I look things remind me of Sweep. I didn't realize how much stuff he left behind. And visualize this one—I took off so fast last summer there are dirty dishes in the sink."

"So what else is new? You've had dirty dishes in the sink for ten years."

"Let's see. The pipes are okay except for the bathtub. By some miraculous stroke of luck the furnace didn't go out over the winter. I put twenty-five thousand miles on the Porsche. I've added about forty pounds since the night I saw you in the dealer lady's apartment and I've started playing the guitar."

"That's what I like about you, Sarah. You always fill up conversation with talk about the weather. I've got a new song, by the way. I'm going to dedicate it to Cyclops."

"Okay. I'll bite. How come?"

"So I can call it *I Only Have Eye For You.*"

"Are you okay, Bailey?"

"Sure. I'm cracking jokes, aren't I?"

I have found a herd of thundering horses far distant at the edge of a vast golden plain. Clouds lie recumbent on a field of Dick-and-Jane blue. My magic boots get fastened at the thigh. The ground retreats beneath my feet like water colors fleeing from a bath.

The horses are nearer now; I am catching up. The ground begins to change. Brown rocks and stumble briars. There is electric pastel powder in the air. I can see the horses! Four sets of six, set dotted frets apart. They are below me in a valley. They approach a glassy lake. There are slips and slides, soft circle noises. I walk along a ridge to the other side of the hill. I have caught a glimpse of sun.

A garden valley stretches out before me: broccoli the size of elm trees, a patch of cauliflower oaks, a row of maples swaying gently in a breeze like mustard greens.

I get cold and hungry sometimes when I play Chestnut's guitar. Putting on a sweater and eating some food helps.


Oh, Lord. I have made a serious miscalculation. I do not know how I can manage to survive this one. I could split from here right now. Just put the Porsche in gear and go. Leave a note on the front door. Drive over to Sandra's. Or even head on down to New York for a day. Take the blasted bottle of lemon-scented bath oil that makes skin feel smooth to the palms. Take a change of clothes. Chestnut's guitar....

It is too late.

I hear the *clump clump clump* of a familiar vehicle coming down the road. There was a time I could identify most every car that passed my house by sound. I will not have the local find me in the bathroom staring at the tub, although my tub is large, antique, on lion-headed legs. It will take me easily. The legs are painted silver grey, the color of old dimes. The outside of the tub is a mottled bluish grey with occasional patches of dull ochre. The color reminds me of a photograph I saw somewhere of a polychrome Kamares-style middle Minoan jar. A spider has constructed quite a nifty web between the pipes that are malfunctioning. The weave of spider webbing proves a tensile strength second only to that of fused quartz.

Hargrove pulls his station wagon into my driveway. I watch him from the bathroom window. He adjusts a blue and tan straight-cut jacket I have not seen before. He runs a comb through his curly blonde hair. He retrieves a tool kit and a bottle in a paper bag from the back seat. He avoids the path to the front door, which is *still* muddy, and enters the garage. He is in the passageway below me. He thinks he knows where he is going.

I descend the stairs and meet him in the kitchen.

"Hello, Hargrove. It's good to see you."

Hargrove stares at me enhaloed. His face fits the space defined by the rim of the large copper bowl on the wall behind him. He puts his tool kit on the round oak table and scratches at his crotch. "I think I've got the crabs," he says.

"I don't want to fuck," I say. "I just want my pipes fixed. I haven't had a bath in a week. I'm definitely ready. See?" I open my bathrobe and expose myself.

I am exactly where I want to be. I have survived my homecoming. My livingroom is neat. My kitchen is in working order. I have caught in traps all thirty-seven of the mice that missed the cracker crumbs upon my bed sheets, although they gnawed shelf edges in the kitchen cabinet. I have packed Sweep's things away and put them in the storage room in the garage: the nineteen-pound white marble ornament we picked up in the Junque and Anteaks Shoppe outside of Marblehead on a trip we made while looking for a house to buy; four cartons filled with magazines and clippings; two dozen well-washed jars with lids, all trace of label glue removed; the suit he swore he'd never wear again. The miscellaneous tools I've put into the tool box and the books and records I have mixed up with my own. The record albums and the books are in alphabetical order, beginning with an oversized cardboard-bound edition of The Ananga Dingle Dangle. No doubt Sweep prides himself on traveling very light.

I am feeling like a self-righteous prig.

I have repaired my drum. It was a chore, obtaining and attaching the new skin, but there are body limits to the time that I can play guitar each day. The calluses forming on my left hand finger tips are not yet strong enough to thoroughly protect against new blisters.

I start it out easy, a soft even beat. There is a rhythm that I strive for which is very hard to find. There is much moisture in the air; the head of a good drum is sensitive to change.

It takes a while to get it going good. I find a new hard-driving pattern with an accent complication, the left hand flirting with the deep voice at the center.

Lips and Hayworth return.

They arrive in the white Lincoln; a third woman is at the wheel. She has backed into my driveway.

"How very good to see you," Lips says. She is wearing a pink spring coat and green galoshes.

"Yes, indeed, we missed your drum," Hayworth says. "You've been gone a long time."

Their smiles are ghastly. They notice there has been a change in me.

"We can't stay today," Lips says apologetically.

"We've come with an invitation," Hayworth says.

"Wednesday evening at six. A pot-luck supper followed by a lecture."

"We would like you to come," Hayworth says.

"Yes. It would be very nice to have you."

Hayworth is diddling around with a white scarf at her neck. The woman behind the wheel of the Lincoln is cleaning her nails with a metal nail file.

"We're having a guest speaker. All the way from Biloxi, Mississippi. The Reverend Simon Washburne. He's very nice," Lips says. She is exercising a small muscle in her right cheek. "We've had him before. He thanks the Good Lord for the new sheep He sends into the fold."

"He uses a blackboard," Hayworth says.

"What for?" I say.

"Why, to show us what hell looks like, of course," Lips says.

I have invested $3.36, and I am really going to do it. I've got it all together now: two paper bags, a box, a turquoise plastic dust pan and a whisk broom, a roll of paper towels and a plastic bottle of spray cleaner. I pull the Porsche out into the driveway. A shaggy-haired, clean-shaven man with a nicely fleshy face and a nose that angles to one side is coming down the road. He has a look of pouchy pockets. I think he is about my age. He has a flute case in his hand.

"You must be David Spofford," I say. "Sam the guitar maker told me about you. I'm Sarah Campbell. Isn't it a beautiful day."

"A gift," David says. He looks at me expectantly. I am wearing the black nappy pants I bought in Aspen and a flowered muu-muu that I picked up at a rummage sale.

"It's my all-purpose super-duper work outfit."

He smiles, and makes no move to leave.

"Look, don't go down to the lake. Stay here and play your flute for me, would you? I'm going to clean out the Porsche."

"Okay. Sure. I'll do that," David says.

I start by opening up the passenger's door.

It is not going to be as bad as I had thought.

It is just going to take time.

David assembles his flute. He acknowledges the birches with a trill; a bit of scale to the thickets. A nod to the pussy willows that have finally appeared. The warm-up exercises coming from his flute are similar to but different from the warm-up exercises Sweep would do. The sound is mostly rich and mellow. I am not surprised. He is wearing comfy khakis rolled up at the ankles; his socks are the same color as the Porsche. His feet are at right angles to each other in the pose that poster painters paint the blue god Krishna.

"What have you got?" he asks.

"A couple of stones I picked up at the Badlands in South Dakota." I hand the stones to David.

"I've been there. Incredible place, isn't it."

"Wild. I was there last August. Maybe September. A flukey day, sort of like this. So bright and clear it seemed not real. I found the place pretty scary, and I almost didn't get into it. I was depressed, which is beside the point. Anyway, I was heading back to the Porsche from the Ranger Station, and there was a fat woman who I thought looked like me walking from the parking area. I only weighed about one eighty then, but felt *fat* because I was feeling guilty. The woman had a spastic teenager with her, a boy dressed in a red and green checked jacket and a pair of green and yellow striped pants and they really freaked me. I walked off the path and headed for the other side of one of those cotton-candy-colored formations and discovered an old gnarled tree you wouldn't have believed."

"A cottonwood?"

"I'm not sure. But whatever the goddamned thing was, how it ever managed to grow there I don't know, and then it started to rain. About twelve seconds of big, separate drops and next thing I knew there was a stream flowing along the base of the tree and the ground turned out to be clay and it was full of these little stones. The clay was sort of a pink color, and it absorbed all of the water in perhaps five minutes. They're really beautiful when they're wet. Come on inside. I'm done with the Porsche. I'll wet these down and make a pot of coffee."

"Sure."

## "You don't say much, do you?"

*The Song of David* for Unaccompanied Flute by Phillip Ramey
Copyright © 1977 by Phillip Ramey.

It is possible to walk down to the lake on solid ground instead of mud at last, and I am wearing my soft leather boots. I found them in a corner of the closet in the small hot room beneath the attic eaves. To get them on and tied was difficult, but it was worth the effort. The soles allow the earth its say.

The mud was much, much worse than the mud last spring, I think. It seems a short time to remember, doesn't it, a year. The walking is no harder now than then. If anything, I move around much more. I take the pace quite slow. Has my perception of it altered? It seems to me I never moved around at all until Chestnut's guitar began to play for me. As if I sat for years.

A bird cruises on an air current, a black speck against the cloudless deep blue sky. It drifts, swoops, divebombs to earth. A bird of prey. It comes up empty clawed. I have whiled away the morning. The sun reads barely noon.

There is the smell of growth in the air. I fill my lungs. I do a little work and achieve a comfortable rhythm. There are stones to kick. The sun is warm upon me.

I put a foot out to the side and transfer my weight; slowly I extend my arms and lift the other leg behind me, bending the support knee. There is a momentary protest from my buried muscles, a quiver of fear that I might fall.

There are ghosts watching in the wind.

I find a balance. I bend my waist, just a bit, then extend up quickly and throw my arms up high. The hind leg follows forward of its own accord and roots on the earth; I arch my back and hold the moment. Then a whirl and six small steps on the balls of my feet, a sweep of an arm to the ground, three jump steps and a click of my heels. The sound of ancient panpipes piping is whirring in my ears.

How I delude myself!

It is not David come to play his flute with me.

It is just the blood rushing to my head.

# Chapter Three

When will it ever end? My left hand aches; the calluses I thought sufficient to protect my fingertips are breaking down. There are indentations like the cracks in coffee beans. I have lost Chestnut's grey plastic pick so there are blisters on my right hand fingertips. When I press them with my thumb they hurt. The muscle which connects my right hand shoulder to the spine just above the small of my back has stiffened up on me. I would like to know what it is called so I can curse it adequately.

I drive to the guitar shop.

Toot-toot! Sam and David are both there.

"What's this muscle called, do you know?" I say. "Nice day, isn't it."

"Christ, Sarah, knock it off," Sam says.

"Oh, come on, Sam. All I said was it's a nice day."

"It's raining the proverbial fuzzies out there!"

"You must be varnishing the new guitar."

"Wrong. I am *not* varnishing the new guitar. Someday someone will ask me for a guitar with a blue tint to the varnish and then we'll have a fucking drought."

"Listen, I've found something new in my tuning. Do you want to listen, or maybe even play?"

"I want to stand at the window and *brood*," Sam says.

"I want to know what that thing is you have in your hand," David says. "It looks like a rejected doorknob."

"I thought no one would ever ask. It used to be my clock. I baked it by mistake. It was making too much noise, so I put it in the oven and forgot about it when I put the broiler on to grill some cheese for lunch. I've started using my fingers instead of a pick and it's not as loud but I'm hearing voices. I think they're in the fifth string."

Sam makes a gesture of exasperation and begins to file the frets on a guitar he should have had repaired in April.

David takes the remains of my clock and begins an inch by inch examination.

I remove Chestnut from her case and adjust the strings.

"The rhythm's all different too," I say. "Sort of syncopated. It's familiar, but I just can't place it."

"Let's hear it," David says.

My fingers walk the strings, like the legs of Disney dwarfs, stiff at first, like an old woman testing out a steel walker. Small aches. A stumble and recovery. A skip and a jump. I find my rhythm and walk a country lane. I pause by the edge of a brook in blue dusk. There! A trout ripple. And another!

There is a bridge across. I arch to balance on the balls of my flesh like a mime walking through a field of mines.

I take the open field on the other side at a gallop, slow to lope. The voices live beyond the dark forest. I find my way to the other side—

"Ah, Sarah," David says. He is smiling with pleasure. "You've got yourself a blues. If you were in the standard tuning, you'd recognize the rhythm easily."

"Christ," Sam says. "That's all she needs to hear. Next week she'll be singing and calling herself Fat Sarah."

Fat Sarah! I can live with that!

"What about the voices on the fifth string?" I say.

"That's the second string," Sam says. "The fifth string is the A string. The second string is the B."

What does he mean? If what I call the fifth string is the second string then it makes what I call the top string the bottom string and that can not be. *I* am at the top when Chestnut begins to play for me.

"The voices are harmonics," David says. "You've got a couple of extra harmonics available to you because of the way you're tuning."

"She's got a warp in her guitar neck, that's what she's got," Sam says. "She's compensated for it by tuning the strings to quarter tones."

"That's right," David agrees. "She's got a very good ear."

"And she's also got the dirtiest, deadest most over-played strings I've ever had in my shop," Sam says. He opens a drawer in his worktable and pulls out a set of strings. Before I can protest, he has taken Chestnut from me and fastened her neck in a vise.

"No, don't! I'll lose my tuning!" He takes a pair of clippers and cuts the strings from the guitar. "You'll get it back," he says.

"How am I going to get it back? How am I going to get it back?"

"She's right," David says. "How's she going to get it back?"

"So she won't get it back," Sam says. "She'll find another one instead. It's time she started playing in the standard tuning anyway."

The standard tuning? Why would anyone want to play in the standard tuning? I am feeling uncontrolled and nearly violent.

"She could do it with a chromatic pitchpipe," David says. "Check each string with a pitchpipe and make a record of the names of the notes."

"Yeah," Sam says. "That's a good idea. Or she could figure out the relationships between the strings."

"That would work too," David says. "The relation-ships would remain constant regardless of the notes."

"Come here, Sarah," Sam says. "Watch the way I'm putting these on. There are other ways of doing it, but I recommend this one. And by the way, you're holding your left hand wrong. It's hard at first, but you've got to turn your wrist this way, at a right angle to the neck, so you'll gain speed up and down and across the fingerboard.''

"Let me try putting on the next string."

"Sure. And then I'm putting your guitar into the standard tuning."

"...so I fiddle around with the strings and find a new tuning almost right away, and they start to play with me and then I find an easy way to hit a chord way up high on Chestnut's neck, using my left hand thumb as a barre across the strings. 'You're fearless,' David says, 'but you play in E minor too much.' 'You can't do that!' Sam says. 'Nobody uses their thumb to barre across the strings.' You don't understand a word of this, do you, Sandra?''

Sandra shrugs. "I understand that it upset you, but it sounds like they were taking you seriously. Maybe they stopped playing because they were tired. Did you ask either of them?"

"No," I said. "I just kept on playing and then I got really strange and started reciting Chestnut's 'Sunny Day Blues' in time to the new tuning. The same song we're listening to. I told the guys she called it a love song. 'That's not a love song,' Sam said and asked us to leave so he could get to work. David came back here because he wanted to hear some of Chestnut's tapes. 'Her playing is erratic,' he said. 'Her ideas are certainly much stronger than her sense of time,' he said. 'She swallows too many of her words,' he said. Then he just up and left. I don't know. I guess it's just me. Sometimes I expect too much. I saw both of them yesterday for a little while and everything was okay. What do you think, Sandra?''

"Don't worry about it," she says. "I'm not so sure I'd call those songs of Chestnut's love songs either, by the way." She is scratching at the rough red scaly patches on her left leg. "You know, the black flies aren't bothering me so much this year. This looks worse than it feels."

"Doesn't Hank mind? It looks awful."

"I don't know, He's never said."

"Black flies. I hate the mother fuckers. They make me swell up and they remind me of Will."

"That's the first time you've mentioned him," Sandra says.

"Yeah, I know. And it's the last time, too. You know, I really don't want to plant this garden. All I want to do is play the guitar. I'm pissed off at Hank for rototilling without asking me. You put him up to it, didn't you?"

"Well, we had to pay rental for a full day anyway, and you were off gallivanting. We did Sam's garden also. Come on. Don't be so lazy. Have you got the seeds?"

Cousin Rachael, my only blood relative, comes for a visit. There are two letters and a call confirming her flight. Cousin Rachael is forty, a spinster of habits. I resign myself and warn her to expect Fat Sarah.

I meet her plane in Boston.

"You look absolutely dreadful," she says in greeting.

Great.

"Why don't you go on a diet?"

"Maria Callas once weighed two hundred and ten pounds," I say hopefully.

"And *what* is that thing you're wearing?"

"It's a gas-station attendant's uniform. I found it at a second-hand store."

"For god's sake!"

"It's comfortable."

"Do you have a sewing machine?"

"Yes."

"Let's get some fabric. You could wear something like a caftan. They're easy to make."

She sweeps the floor each morning and she bathes three times a day.

She washes ashtrays when they've been soiled by just a single butt.

She talks incessantly about her boss, a man she has devoted all her time to now for nearly twenty years.

The toilet breaks down in anxiety.

I am not about to go another Hargrove round with Cousin Rachael in the house.

I explain about the woods.

I am blamed for the plumbing failure.

She uses my car to drive the half-mile to the gas station each day and shortens her visit to a week.

Cousin Rachael sure knows about bending time.

June 15th? How did it get to be June 15th?

*June 15, 1972*

*Dear Sweep:*

*I have received the letter from your lawyer, and although he specifically requested that I direct my answer to him, what I have to say does not need to be filtered through an intermediary.*

*I find the idea of divorce extremely painful, but no worse than this strange limbo state of legal separation. So I will sign any papers that need signing, and I will put no obstacles in your way.*

*As to the matter of alimony. It had not occurred to me, although it has obviously occurred to you. Why would I ask for alimony? I have the money from my inheritance, which will last me another few years if I am frugal, and when I do need money, I will go out and work for it. That's the way I've always been, and getting divorced won't change things.*

*That's all. Except to let you know that I have not changed my mind about the drum.*

*Best,*
*Sarah*

David looks different to me every time I see him, although his clothes remain essentially the same. There is the three-quarter length navy raincoat, a soft green flannel shirt, a pair of dark green corduroys, the khakis that he wears rolled up, a purple long-sleeved jersey blazoned *Thunder-bird* across his chest. I like it when he wears that. It means his flute is playing high for him.

There is just a single light on in the Broadman's house as I drive up, and I do not hear the radio that David usually keeps going while he works. He has not told me much about the book that he is writing, except to say "it is essentially a plotless novel; I am concerned directly with the feel of things."

"Hey, I like that," he says. I am wearing the red caftan that Cousin Rachael trimmed with purple braid.

"It's my new uniform. I've got three of them. Made with my own two hands. I wasn't sure you were home. Are you testing out your hearing and night vision?"

"What happened?" David puts a finger on the pimple near the corner of my mouth. I had resisted it for a day and a half.

"Ouch. Lost control," I say. "It's a throwback. I used to do it all the time. This is the first damage I've done to my face in months. Congratulate me."

"Congratulations."

"Want to play? I just happen to have Chestnut the Magnificent with me."

"Nope."

Tonight he wears his red striped shirt and grey sweat pants. I am beginning to understand the sweat pants.

"I'm beginning to understand the sweat pants. Sometimes you play when you wear them but mostly you want to talk. They must be uncomfortable."

"You're crazy," he says. "Do you want a drink?"

"Sure."

He makes us gin and tonics. He squeezes juice from a fresh lime.

"I got to thinking about some traveling today," David says. "Ulan Bator, Mongolia, perhaps. Or Kuala Lumpur, Malaysia. Tegucigalpa, Honduras. Nouakchott, Mauritania. Atuna in the Marquesas of French Polynesia. Or maybe Bujumbura, Burundi."

I think about that.

"What do you think?" David says.

"*Son of Flubber* is a very funny movie."

"What Trenton Makes the World Takes."

"What?"

"Aren't we playing non sequiturs?"

"Oh, I see. No. It's just that I got stuck in a place called Willetsburg, Colorado a couple of months back, bored, bored, bored, and *Son of Flubber* was playing at the only movie theater."

"So?"

"You suddenly reminded me of Fred McMurray. That's a pretty good movie, by the way. It's about power people trying to take away something that can put people on the elevator rides, this peculiar stuff that Fred McMurray has developed as a chemist that lets things bounce, I think, or fly. I can't remember that—that's not the kind of thing I remember—just the nice metaphor of it."

"It doesn't sound funny."

"Well, the laughs are painful. They're provided by a kind of role exaggeration that takes the power people and exposes them so the humanness can be seen. The audience laughed, and I did too, because the roles were so removed from everyday reality: chemists, and flyers, and army brass, and communications and advertising people, people with real power wanting something. But the chemists and pilots and army brass weren't in the audience. They're not the people who laugh at *Son of Flubber,* because they want to be the people who are exposed on the screen. I'm sorry. I seem to be rambling on. I don't know why I'm doing that. I usually don't talk like this. I don't like myself very much when I ramble on. Say something."

"Did you know that there are less than a thousand miles of surfaced roads in Mongolia?"

# Chapter Four

Five for July 4th dinner. I hope there is going to be enough:

*Steamed Pork Dumplings*
*Hot and Sour Soup*
*Chicken braised in Soy Sauce flavored with*
*   Star Anise*
*Ground Beef and Oysters*
*Shrimps in Spicy Red Sauce*
*Cold Cucumber Salad*

Sam is trying out the beautiful Brazilian rosewood and mahogany guitar he finished making yesterday. It has a strange and hollow, full, full sound. He will not play my guitar when I have it in an open tuning. David plays his flute. Hank is working out upon my drum.

"Can I help?" Sandra joins me in the kitchen.

"Sure," I say. "You know, I used to do this a lot when Sweep and I were married."

"Peel shrimps?"

"Sure. But I meant be off in the kitchen cooking, or making coffee while the men were playing ja-*az*."

"It sounds like you resented it."

"No, I didn't. I liked listening, and I never thought about playing an instrument then. Sweep's musician

friends were all men except for one gal who played piano
and a couple of singers.''

"I can't play anything," Sandra says.

"What about the bass drum?''

"Ye gads, Sarah, that didn't have anything to do with
music. I don't know what it had to do with, except stealing
my time. Mama's family was involved with General
William Booth all the way back at the beginning in
England in the eighteen sixties and putting in some
Salvation Army time became a family tradition. They do
good things, but I wasn't given a choice. If Hank and I ever
decide to have kids I won't force them into it, although
Mama would turn over in her grave.''

"You really did that, didn't you. Stand on street
corners in Philadelphia and bang on a bass drum.''

"Sure. Somebody had to do it. It was kind of
interesting. I blocked it out and dreamed of becoming a
New York City Radio City Music Hall Rockette." She rolls
the title on her tongue like a ripe Muscatel grape. "Mostly I
did secretarial work, though. Bang bang on the drum, then
bang bang on the typewriter.''

I could stand a little bang bang. David brought a
Mateus wine bottle for me to practice with, a practical first
step in learning how to play a flute. It is green like a jewel,
and it feels good in my hands. There is a paper collar
around the bottle's neck and it wears a pendant with the
word *sogrape* in a frame. I blow air across the mouth of the
bottle until I am light headed, but I can not find the sound.
If all else fails, I can stick it up my cunt.

It is very late.

The others are all gone.

David is in the bed in the spare room, asleep. Surely he
lies on his back. My best lovers have all learned to sleep on
their backs. Perhaps one arm is at his side, the other
crooked above his head. The music that we made tonight
excited me. There is a rightness to the music of his phallic
flute and my female-shaped guitar. My body feels caressed,
as my body did the night I watched Will run his hands

across the clay that he had made into a work of art by looking at me.

I would like to go to David in the hot room beneath the attic eaves, but surely I can not. He is afraid of me. I think he fears he does not know the proper way to make love to my body.

We are all the same: two breasts, a navel, clitoris and cunt, an anus, pair of knees, a neck and hair, two arms, a belly, back and thighs, two feet and feelings stuffed, encased, in skin.

Our bodies are all padded cells.

I would crawl into the bed and feel him wrap me in his arms, the shock of flesh and flesh.

My body knows that I am ready.

There is a hot wet warmth where hot wet warmth should be.

I wish that he would find the courage now to come to me.


"You look like you haven't slept in a week," Sandra says. "What gives?"

"I've been singing."

"Good for you!"

"All of sudden, in the middle of the night the other night, I started to sing Chestnut's 'Lost in the Heaven' song. I just opened up and let my voice fill the center of the music. I haven't sung since high school. I don't know how any adult learns how to sing. I scared myself. If anyone had been walking around outside my house they would have thought a wolf was howling in my livingroom, and then I realized that I'm not Chestnut and I have other things to say, and I started coming up with some words of my own and....Why do I make things so hard for myself, Sandra?"

"I don't know."

"I'm in love with David."

"I know," she says.

"You know? How do you know?"

"It's obvious. It shows all over the place."

"I'm going to get hurt."

"It always hurts, doesn't it?"

"Yeah, I guess so."

She makes us coffee and we go sit in the sun. The black flies have gone away at last and the mosquitoes are in hiding until dusk.

"I haven't slept with him," I say.

"Why not?"

"He hasn't asked me."

Sandra laughs. "You've changed, Sarah. That never used to stop you."

"Yeah, I know, But this is different."

"Why?"

"Because he listens to me and because he takes me seriously and because I want *him*, not just a fuck, and he's going to say no if I ask."

"Are you sure?"

"No, I'm not absolutely sure, but I think so."

"There's only one way to find out," she says.

"Yeah, I know."

"Sarah?"

"Yes?"

"Put on some perfume, and wear that brown print caftan Rachael made. You're really very beautiful, you know."


"Play for me, David. So that I can hear your song. I can't hear your song if we're always playing my music."

"I thought that's what you wanted," he says.

"Right now I have a need for something to respond to."

"Do I get a hint of the mood?" he says. "What kind of rhythm do you want me to play?"

I shake my head. It is no more words I want. We are in the Broadman's livingroom. I am sitting on the couch. We have been arguing significances.

David begins to play his flute. He is being gentle. That is good. I am about to offer myself as the fat of the land.

How many Biafran children could have made it on my belly flab?

I catch his song on Chestnut's brand new G string. I am uncomfortable sitting on the couch. My muscles are very lazy. I follow David's scale progression. It is different from the way I normally would play. It leads me to a chord I did not know. It suggests a rhythm that I like. One and two and three and four and pause, one, two. One and two and three and four and pause, one, two. One and two and three and four and pause, one, two. It feels like speed. I get under it and ride the wave...rain forests on the flank....

"I love you, David."

"Yes, I know."

"Let's make love."

"I'm going back to Boston day after tomorrow. My book is nearly done."

"I'm not asking for a commitment."

"Look, I know that. But what we have goes beyond sex, don't you think?"

"Oh, fuck. *Damn* you. Go away. I thought I had it all figured out. I'm sorry I said anything. You're right. Friends are important, and we make good music together. The feelings are essentially the same, and there isn't any mess, and you don't have to worry about whether or not you can figure out how to make love to my body. Well, that's okay. I don't know how to make love in this body anyway. I haven't been with a man once in nearly a year, did you know that? And I've got my period anyway. Stop it. Don't touch me. Go away."

"You're crying, Sarah."

"I'm not crying. I don't cry. Me? Sarah Fay Cohen Campbell? Never. It would fuck up my act."

"I don't want to hurt you."

"You can't hurt me. I only hurt myself. The vibes are physical. I trust it. This is the place of choice." I have worked up a blister on the bottom of my right hand little finger. What is it complaining about? It's had a free ride most of its life.

"No. Don't do that. Put down your guitar, Sarah."

"Not until you put down your flute."

"Look, I'm sorry I'm being clumsy. I don't know how to approach you. That blasted thing you're wearing. There's so much of you. Don't laugh. I'm being as honest as I can."

"I wasn't laughing. I was just remembering how awful it was when I was a teen-ager and really didn't know what to do, no experience to draw on and I didn't know who I was or what anything was supposed to feel like and it doesn't make any difference, does it, the feelings are the same."

"Do you always get what you want, Sarah?"

"No."

The Porsche is not quite ready. I have given up a day for it to be serviced. The windshield wipers weren't doing their job. The timing was off. I had not had the oil changed for thousands of miles.

There is a small waiting room off to one side of the garage, with a grey tweed carpet, red molded plastic chairs and two amber glass ashtrays in brass-colored pedestals. There is a Coke machine, a candy machine, a pile of useless magazines: *Car and Driver, Sports Illustrated, Popular Mechanics.*

A little girl in dungarees and a dirty white sweater approaches the candy machine. She selects a box of Milk Duds. She sits on one of the chairs.

"Dum da de dum dah," the little girl says in a deep voice. She extracts a candy with a wet index finger. She closes the box. "How nice to meet you, Charlie." Charlie Milk Dud disappears into her mouth. She shakes the box and transfers it to the other hand.

She looks up. "I'm playing," she says. "You don't watch me, okay?"

"Okay." I thumb a magazine. There is an article about Rod Gilbert.

"Dum da de dum dah, I'm looking for Fred." The little

girl wets her index finger and inserts it into the box. She closes the lid. "Oh, Fred," she whines, "what is this bump? Is there something the matter with your leg? No? Okay." Fred Milk Dud disappears. She shakes the box and transfers it to the other hand.

Rod Gilbert zips down the ice and fakes out Jean Beliveau. Is he going to score the goal? I find the continued-on page. It is half gone. Someone has torn out the coupon for a trial pair of latex jockey shorts.

"Dum da de dum dah. Oh, it's you, Ernie. How is Burt today? Fine? Good. Good-bye." Exit Ernie. The little girl fucks up her ritual. She shakes the box but has forgotten to close the lid. She jumps up from her chair and passes the buck.

"Oh, no," she says, arms on her hips, an angry pout on her lips. *"I told you guys to stay in the box."*

"Would you like that, Sarah?" Bailey says. "Would it feel good?"

"Yes."

He kneels before me; he strokes my thighs with gentle hands. "Ask me," he says. "Say the words."

His palms trace lines of ice upon my flesh. I close my legs and rearrange my brown print caftan. "I can't," I say.

Bailey moves to settle back in the stuffed chair, arms up and clasped behind his head. I put Chestnut away in her case. He chuckles. "Ah, Sarah, you're sure a strange one," he says. "You go through such changes."

"I'm out of practice. I've been celibate for a very long time. Real contact is different from imaginary contact. I've lost touch with it. I've forgotten how to play the game. I drove all the way down to New York to share my music with you. I wanted you to like what I'm doing, the sound of my guitar, although I realize—"

"Why you idiotic cunt," Bailey says. *"Look* at me. I come home after a 3-hour workout on a goddamned radio commercial because I haven't written a decent song in months and I find this very heavy apparition waiting for me who calls herself Sarah and proceeds to give me such a performance my cock stands up in salute and she wants *words.*"

"That's right. Sometimes I need words. I'm not a mind reader. I only know the feelings that I feel."

"Okay, I'll give you words. The way you're playing that guitar after only a couple of months is sca-ry. I always knew you were stubborn, but I didn't think you could ever discipline yourself. The music is strong and exciting and some of it is startling, especially toward the end there, when you were hitting those harmonics and half singing, half reciting the words to Chestnut's love songs, and you damn well....Stop grinning like a Cheshire cat, my dear, or I'll sing you the commercial I wrote this afternoon and demand words from you."

"You are very dear to me, Bailey."

"Sure I am. That's why you're here. Good Old Bailey. Always available on the rebound or when you're horny and can't have the guy you want. I know you, Sarah. At least this David doesn't sound like a total schnook. Come on. I'll take you out for a steak and then, by god, I'm going to make love to you. We've both earned it. And by the way, a friend of mine named Cliff Ross has rented a place just about ten miles from your house for the summer. He's a guitar player. He's got a couple of other musicians with him. They're trying to...oh, *Sar*ah, what an exciting thing to *do*...."

"Which hand do you use to jerk off with?"

"Both," he says. "I pump with my right and hold the balls with my left."

"Do it," I say.

He moves my hand to his thick hard cock. "Feel what you do to me," he says.

"Changed my mind," I say. "Fuck me, Bailey."

The door is answered by a portly, dark-haired unsmiling man. He runs me down with steam-roller eyes. I know the look. I have used it on Lips and Hayworth.

"Hi, my name's Sarah," I say. I shift Chestnut to my other arm. "I'm a friend of Bailey Gorsham's. I've been fooling around with some open guitar tunings, and I'm looking for people to play with. Would you like to play? Are you Cliff Ross? You look so stern. Am I crashing a private party? Should I go away? Do I need a password?"

"No. Okay. Enough. I know Bailey. Come on in. I'm Bill."

There is a full set of rock and roll drums in the livingroom, a conga drum, a couple of microphones, music stands, two amplifiers, an enormous bright red electric guitar resting in a green upholstered chair. Chestnut is small and needs a polish and I have accidentally gouged the wood on her face with my new pick, which is blue with a ridged top and sometimes makes a sound like a castanet.

There is a gorgeous redhead in the kitchen. He is in his early twenties and wears a short-sleeved T-shirt with rolled up cuffs, exposing magnificent symmetrical biceptual knockers.

"Here's a good one, buddy," Bill says by way of introduction. "She says her name is Sarah. She's a friend of Bailey's. She's playing open tunings on whatever is in that painted cardboard case and she wants to play with lucky us."

"Cool it, Bill," the redhead says.

"Nice to meet you, Buddy," I say.

Bill snorts. I have heard the sound on occasion before.

"My name's Cliff," the redhead says.

"I'll tell you what," I say. "How about if you offer me some of that grass I smell, or smoke some of mine, and let's try this one again."

"Good idea," Cliff says. "Glad to meet you. Don't mind Bill. He's in a real funk. You have to watch out for drummers."

"Is that electric guitar inside yours?"

"Yes," Cliff says. He passes me a joint laced with hash. Why are we sitting here in silence?

"Look," I say. "I'm really up for playing. I've got

something to say with my guitar, but I'm very new at trying
to play with other people and I sure don't understand the
etiquette of getting from here to the place where the music
is."

"Well, that's easy," Cliff says. Easy? Easy? "Just break
out your axe and play. I'll play with you if I like what
you're doing. And el groucho here will also."

"Lay off me, Cliff," Bill says.

"I'll go tune up."

Getting Chestnut tuned quite often makes me nervous.
I can not always tell which strings are sharp and which are
flat. Sam says that is a common ailment. I park myself on a
stool in a corner and check in with my pitchpipe. My caftan
falls quite nicely to the floor. My hair is clean and feels soft
against my cheek.

I get my rhythm pattern going. I play out the chords,
the melody line, the riff that I have learned. I repeat it once,
and once again. Is this going to be a spectacle?

"She's in the D mode," a voice says finally. What does
that mean? It means the sound of an electric guitar—an
electric guitar!—has found me! Now Bill the drummer
makes some sassy passes at his snare drum; he pinches at
his cymbal's bottom. "Tricky little bitch," I hear him say,
"I've got you!" And he hits it then, and I am free.

I find an accent to the rhythm pattern I had not found
before. I investigate a new chord possibility. I find a strum
to accent on the high thin note the snare drum makes on
every other beat. Another to a note I hear, electric,
twanging, every now and then. My beating foot begins to
cramp. I shift positions. I find a sneaky way of getting to a
chord change I can otherwise not reach. There is a rasping
sound to use as a bridge. It is unusual and harsh. It requires
my fingers to go out of position. No one will notice that
I'm not hitting the strings right. Ha, ha, ha.

I am clanged a warning by the cymbals.

I back away and find myself to listen to. There is a trio
of young girls clip clopping Double Dutching jumprope
barreing four strings at the seventh and ninth frets...a

melody line is taking form, somewhere lower middle range. It is caressing me in mellow! I get on top of it and ride the wave...magenta purple cock....I open my eyes.

An albino is playing an electric bass.

He greets me with a nod and a smile.

I had not heard him come into the room, but I can hear him now.

The pick has nearly worked free of my fingers. I am allowed to rest. I find my home riff, play it through, wind down and out.

Will they never be done?

"Hey, Strank, old buddy," Bill the drummer says. "What gives? You come in last and you stop first."

"I stopped first."

"I think I can use some of that in the 'Wichita' song," Bill says. He is most definitely ignoring me. How can he ignore me? "In that bridge we were having trouble with. What do you think?" He plays out my rhythm pattern with a slight variation. Cliff picks up a guitar melody that is not mine; Strank the bass player joins the play. I can not find the notes on my guitar. There are dues to pay for being a beginner playing in an open tuning. It is a con. It lets me play guitar so long as other people will get off upon my energy.

The conga drum is by my side. Toot-toot! I find an easy rhythm and come in to join their song. I trust it when the voices in a drum speak out for me. I close in upon the center.

"Br-a-a-sh! Br-a-a-sh!" the cymbals say.

I have invaded space.

I withdraw to ride the high thin voices at the bright green edge...they sing the rhythm of my song...they lead me to the brink of silence...there is dark power in the center of this mighty drum...this mighty drum...this mighty drum... this mighty drum....

Bill crashes down and stops the play.

Anger!

Red heat!

I can not control the stoppage of the play!

"Hey, jock, don't look now, but your fly is showing," I say. "You got off on my energy, why aren't you letting me play?"

Cliff stops the play.

Strank stops the play.

"I don't know where that chick's head is at," Bill the drummer says.

The midnight energy drainers have caught up with me. They surround my space and push in upon the walls. How did they find me here? Angry, red-faced clacking things, truncated at the knees, they are much too big. They will not let me form the features of their faces. They laugh.

I defend myself and close my eyes. I curl into a ball. I have been here before, and I know what I must do.

I shrink.

I admit it!

Sometimes I am afraid of the dark.

# Chapter Five

Sandra calls. "How's your garden?" she says.

"It's a mess. I've been blaming the hornet's nest in that larch tree beyond the tiger lily bed—I treat hornets with great respect—but actually I've been lazy. I've lost the carrots and broccoli to the weeds and the eggplant to the zucchini."

"I warned you about that," she says.

"Yeah, I know. Four hills didn't sound like much. It's like a dirty joke. Zucchini is going to conquer the world."

"It's pretty good fried in butter with fresh dill, or raw in salads, or in soup."

"I did some with chicken livers and scallions in the wok, and made a great casserole with hunks of lamb and lemon rind."

"I'm down in the dumps. Hank's off visiting his sister. He won't be back until Friday. Invite me over for dinner and I'll do in the hornet's nest for you."

"Sure."

She comes at seven with a jar of kerosene and a long tapered candle. "I thought you'd like this." She hands me a neatly typed index card:

### The Ex-Salvation Army Drummer's Distillery

Cut the top off an overgrown zucchini biggie and scoop out the seeds with a long-handled teaspoon. Be careful to leave the bottom of the shell intact. Stuff the cavity with granulated brown sugar. Replace the top and fasten with toothpicks. Place in a net bag and punch holes in the bottom with a sterilized two-penny nail. Hang over a pan to collect the liquid. Replace brown sugar when needed.

"I think I'll opt out of this one," I say. "It's got to be illegal."

I have blended a cucumber, zucchini and chicken soup to a puree with cream for serving chilled and baked four 4-inch parboiled peeled zucchini stuffed with ricotta, mozzarella, tomatoes and pepperoni.

For dessert we have the hornet's nest. It's the size of a coconut-shaped basketball, grey the color of well-dented garbage cans. The surface texture looks snake scaly from a distance. Sandra douses the hornet's nest with kerosene and sets it on fire. It burns for a long time. Hornets seek the safety of their nest against the dark of night and will never come out. They smack and crackle. The larch tree bears a scar. It will survive. The larch is the oldest tree known to man.

"Can I come in?" Strank the albino says.
"Sure."
He has his bass and a portable amplifier.
"This is a nice place," he says.
"It's funky, but I like it."
"I've been thinking about you a lot," he says. "It was a heavy scene, that jam session at Bill's house. I was involved, and I wasn't involved, and I know I got off on your energy, which means Bill and Cliff did too. We've been playing together for a long time. I read them pretty well. No one was trying to drain you, though to some

extent I think I understand your anger. I don't think it had to do with your being a woman, by the way. I think it had to do with musicianship and experience and the fact that the sound of a conga drum just isn't right in 'Wichita.' "

How can the sound of a conga drum not be right in Wichita? Not enough trees? Wrong color skin? Albinos are not easy things to look at in the light of day.

"I'm sorry. I don't think I can talk about it yet. It was a very painful experience."

"You know, when I first started looking for people to play with—six or seven years ago, I guess—I picked up a couple of guys out hitchhiking because one of them was playing a jew's harp and I drove a hundred miles out of my way because I thought we were going to make music. I wasn't playing the bass then, I was playing the fiddle. We ended up in a fleabag called The Hotel Winner. This was in the coal-mining country of Pennsylvania. They beat me up—I've still got some yellow splotches on my back; my skin is pretty sensitive—broke my fiddle and took my fifty-seven dollars."

"That's some story. I suppose you're saying that I was lucky getting off so easy?"

"Nope. Not at all. I got a damned good song out of the experience. Sold it to Johnnie Cash and I've made nearly fifteen grand on royalties. Is that the guitar you were playing?"

"Yes."

"That's strange. I thought it was full concert size."

Sam seems to take some pleasure in the progress I am making with technique on my guitar now that I work out daily in the standard tuning, although he still thinks I do not know how to play except when we are playing and he forgets what he doesn't know.

"You know, Sam, you were the only one of the guys last summer I didn't sleep with," I say. "How come?"

"I don't know, Sarah. Maybe it's because I thought you needed at least one friend."

"Some friend! All you ever do is give me exercises that feel like work—I'm going nuts with this six string barre exercise. Twenty-four notes at each of the frets. One time up, one time down, rest the outraged muscles near the thumb of my hand."

"The pain's good," Sam says. "It means you're learning to use new muscles and doing it right. I told you you'd be able to get yourself going in the standard tuning. Next you've got to start running your scales."

Running scales?

Why would anyone want to run scales?


I pick up a child's glockenspiel at a rummage sale for 25¢, marked down from half a buck. It is yellow plastic the shape of an Egyptian mummy case with tarnished metal sounding bars held in place by yellow plastic pegs. The sounding device is wood; the head is the size of a penny bubblegum ball, pink the color of Indian country in the setting sun. It is impaled on a yellow Sugar Daddy stick.

The sound is very tinny. I work through "Row, Row, Row Your Boat." Is there another way to approach a glockenspiel?

I find a nice rhythm by hitting the metal edge with the side of the wooden stick and the keys with the round sounder. It is beginning to make an Oriental sound. Wouldn't a tabla sound nice. Or a flute.

I spend thirty-seven minutes of my life playing a child's glockenspiel. How is it possible to justify the indulgence?


Bailey and I are in a silly mood. We have pulled the blinds, locked the doors and play together in the bathtub.

"Have you ever done that before?" I ask.

"What?"

"Peed like you did a while ago?"

"Now, Sarah, you're a big girl. Don't say pee. Say urinate."

"Bless you. That's the best advice I've had in a long time. Now be serious, and tell me what to do."

"About what?"

"Oh, the monetary crisis, or the crumbling beams, or if I should do the Boston thing, or whether or not I should shave my legs—"

"Yes."

"—or under my arms—"

"No."

"—or why I still get haunted sometimes by the—"

"What's the Boston thing?"

"A friend of Sam's runs a club which opens to new talent twice a month. It sounds like just the place for me. Anything goes. A strict time limit is the only rule. I could do one of Chestnut's songs, and I've got my blues, and a mostly-music song in the standard tuning. I can stretch it out to twenty minutes. If I don't get scared and freeze up, that is. And besides, David's there."

"How about some more hot water?" Bailey says. "That ought to help."

"Are these stretch marks from a child, Sarah?" Strank says.

"Yes."

"You've never mentioned a child."

"It was stillborn. A boy."

"I'm sorry." He bends his head and gently runs his tongue across my belly.

Oh, Strank. You sure are scary.

Who am I kidding? There is no way to cheat. Either you find it or you don't.

I give up. The little finger of my left hand has gone numb. I am unable to make a fist. I have pounded on the drum head for an hour. I can not find the mystery.

Lips and Hayworth pull into the drive. They are in the Lincoln. They have been pretty kind. They have left me alone for a long time.

"Hello, today." It is Hayworth. She must be in a good mood. She is wearing a printed sundress with a hem that comes almost up to her knees.

"Hello, today," I reply. It is 3:30 in the afternoon and I have been nipping at the gin. It's as adequate an excuse as any.

"Hello," Lips says. She smiles. Naturally. "It looks like it's going to clear up, don't you think?"

Pretty sneaky dame. She forces me to look outside. I stick my head out the door. "I don't know. Maybe," I say.

"Well, you know what they say," Lips says. "May-Bees don't fly all the year long."

It is time to get rid of Lips and Hayworth.

"Did your mother punish you for masturbating when you were children?" I say.

David doesn't come, although I called and gave him two weeks' notice.

I give the performance anyway.

I wear a caftan and the old-prom-dresses patchwork scarf that Sandra made for me for luck. The dresses were the only thing I let her salvage as I burned memento moris of my past: letters from old beaus, the correspondence with my mother that took place the years I spent in college, the photo album that contained the pictures of my father, a stranger growing older as the baby girl he held attained each yearly change toward six. The scarf is an interesting example of the transformation of the stuff of pain into a pleasure tangible.

There are more than thirty people in the audience, and I am last of five to play.

Will I ever learn the things that I must learn to be a satisfactory performer? Why is it not enough to show that I can use my fingers and my voice together? That is every bit as difficult as writing different white chalk messages with each of one's two hands.

I do not understand how they could so expose themselves—the one who stood up here and showed that he had mastered circle movements of the torso and the waist, the one who practiced variations on the flexing of the knees, the one who so disguised the task of walking that it looked like play, the one who simply showed that it was possible to stand instead of sit.

It is only when I need to look to find a chord change when I also sing the words of Chestnut's songs that I can even manage pulling up the lids which, blessed mercy, cover up my eyes.

It is full moon. I walk down to the lake. A storm is brewing and the mosquitoes do not bother me. I do not understand about the passing of the time. It is my birthday once again. Thirty-four years old. Thirty-four years old. Thirty-four years old. What does that mean? A year ago tonight I was in Iowa, I think, or perhaps in Minnesota. Two years ago tonight I was still a faithful wife. Three years ago tonight I was still in love with Sweep. Who will love me as I am?

The music has gone very well today.

I have learned how to make a trill on the second string of my guitar. I found it accidentally, although of course I knew that it was there. Musicians have known about it for centuries. It is a better use for an index finger than pulling the trigger of a Ruger.

How has it gotten out of whack again? It seems to happen every seven days. I take a look around my livingroom. The jacket for the Allman Brothers album I have bought is on the floor on top of Tuesday's paper. The table is a cluttered mess: a brandy glass, two coffee mugs, the sugar bowl that Ernest made for me, a box of Ritz crackers, three of Chestnut's tapes, an ashtray, two letters, an empty pack of Bambu cigarette papers, two broken picks.

I pick up the mess in the livingroom and make myself a shopping list. It is time for an excursion. I have been out of toothpaste for several days. Dentyne only goes so far.

I walk the aisles slowly and select things for my cart: a *Family Circle* with a dynamite dessert display on the cover, skinless Portuguese sardines, a jar of sweet-pickled cauliflower, six wrapped-in-cellophane homemade wholewheat flour donuts, two fine-looking packages of meaty short ribs which I will marinate in soy and honey, mustard and garlic and bake in the oven.

There is a long line at the check-out. I do not mind. There is no rush now. Chestnut will wait for me. She isn't going anywhere.

A plump little girl faces me in her grocery-cart seat. She is scrubbed with Windex, and wears pink ribbon bows above each ear.

"You're fat," she says.

"That's right."

The mother's retreat is blocked by the cart in front and mine behind.

The little girl smiles. I smile back. The mother opens her mouth to scream.

"The god guy is very scary, you know," the little girl says. "He lives in a place over bumps."

The mother closes her mouth, vibrates, then giggles shrilly at her now-revealed Nerwianthic bipod.

"I bet you wish you'd never seen her before," I say to the mother.

"Boy, you can say that again," the mother says. She admonishes her daughter. "Shelly, when we get home, I'm going to murder you."

The little girl sticks out a healthy-looking tongue.

# FICTION COLLECTIVE

## books in print:

*Reruns* by Jonathan Baumbach
*Museum* by B. H. Friedman
*Twiddledum Twaddledum* by Peter Spielberg
*Searching for Survivors* by Russell Banks
*The Secret Table* by Mark Mirsky
*98.6* by Ronald Sukenick
*The Second Story Man* by Mimi Albert
*Things In Place* by Jerry Bumpus
*Reflex and Bone Structure* by Clarence Major
*Take It or Leave It* by Raymond Federman
*The Talking Room* by Marianne Hauser
*The Comatose Kids* by Seymour Simckes
*Althea* by J. M. Alonso
*Babble* by Jonathan Baumbach
*Temporary Sanity* by Thomas Glynn
*φ Null Set* by George Chambers
*Amateur People* by Andrée Connors
*Moving Parts* by Steve Katz
*Find Him!* by Elaine Kraf
*The Broad Back of the Angel* by Leon Rooke
*The Hermetic Whore* by Peter Spielberg
*Encores for a Dilettante* by Ursule Molinaro
*Fat People* by Carol Sturm Smith
*Meningitis* by Yuriy Tarnawsky
*Statements 1,* an anthology of new fiction (1975)
*Statements 2,* an anthology of new fiction (1977)

available at bookstores
or from
GEORGE BRAZILLER, INC.